CIRCLES

ALSO BY MARILYN SACHS

CIRCLES

by Marilyn Sachs

DUTTON CHILDREN'S BOOKS   NEW YORK

Library of Congress Cataloging-in-Publication Data

Sachs, Marilyn.
   Circles / by Marilyn Sachs.
     p. cm.
   Summary: Two high school classmates—an aspiring actress and an amateur astronomer—struggle with the changes in their lives, unaware that these changes are leading them to each other.
   ISBN 0-525-44683-4
   [1. Single-parent family—Fiction. 2. Theater—Fiction. 3. High schools—Fiction. 4. Schools—Fiction.] I. Title.
PZ7.S1187Ci 1991   90-37516
[Fic]—dc20   CIP
                                         AC

Published in the United States by Dutton Children's Books, a division of Penguin Books USA Inc.

Editor: Ann Durell

Printed in U.S.A.   First
Edition   10 9 8 7 6 5 4 3 2 1

With love to my granddaughter, the "peerless"
Miranda,
and with thanks for improving and expanding our
family circle.

1

"I didn't get the part," Beebe said. She leaned against the door, and waited.

"You didn't get the part?" her mother repeated. She turned slowly in her chair, fastened her eyes on Beebe's face, and waited.

Beebe tried to avoid looking at her mother's face, at the pain sure to be spreading down from her eyes to her mouth. The pattern was always the same.

"No," she said quickly. "Jennifer Evans got it." With a false and exhausting show of enthusiasm, Beebe added, "She was very good. I'm Lady Montague, and I can also be Juliet's understudy if I want. I'll probably do it. I know a lot of the part already, so I may as well. Mrs. Kronberger said I could try out for the nurse, but I knew I wouldn't get that. Rebecca

Chin got it. She always gets the funny parts. And besides, I wouldn't want to be the nurse anyway." She was chattering away nervously. She knew she was, and she tried to stop herself but she couldn't.

"But . . . but . . . you knew the part perfectly, and you sounded . . . I thought . . ." The disappointment in her mother's voice was heavy and familiar. Every time Beebe had tried out for a leading part, and failed to get it, there invariably followed the scene with her mother afterwards.

In a way, that was the worst part. Her mother suffered so much over her lack of success that she felt squeezed and flattened. Like a pressed duck, she often thought, seeing them hanging up in Chinese groceries.

"I get to wear a stunning green gown with a tight-fitting cap, covered with gold braid and pearls. It's funny how they have the costumes already even though they don't have all the parts filled."

Her mother shook her head and waved a hand angrily downwards. She wasn't interested in costumes. She was interested only in why Beebe hadn't gotten the leading part. Why she never got the leading part.

Sometimes Beebe also wondered. But usually she was too worried about how to break the news to her mother to think about anything else. Sometimes, even before she actually tried out for a role, she would already be worried about consoling her mother and acting cheerful over being rejected.

Ever since third grade, when she had tried out for the part of the girl in *The Night Before Christmas* and had only succeeded in being picked for one of Santa's reindeer, there had been the scene afterwards with her mother. And always, her mother's grief and disappointment seemed deeper than her own.

Beebe stopped talking suddenly, took a few deep breaths, and tried to summon up the standard words of comfort she generally offered to her mother—like a bouquet of wilted flowers. They included ". . . next time . . . said I was really very good . . . don't really mind . . . not really important . . . too much homework anyway this term . . ."

But first her mother had to speak those few bitter words that included ". . . don't know real talent when they see it . . . one of those teacher's pets . . . mother probably president of the PTA . . ."

Beebe waited as her mother's eyes narrowed and her lips parted across her clenched teeth. How pretty her mother was, she thought, even with her face so tight and angry. Her mother should have been an actress, would have been an actress, too, if she hadn't met and married Beebe's father. She had acted leading parts in a whole bunch of school and summer-stock plays, and was playing Beatrice in *Much Ado About Nothing* that summer when they had met.

"He was so sweet," she told Beebe. "He had seen me act. . . ." Whenever Beebe's mother talked about that summer, her face brightened. "He came with some of his friends to the play. One of them lived in Sonoma. That's why he was there in the first place. It's so funny how so many things in life are like that. If his friend didn't live up there, and if he didn't come to visit him, and if somebody hadn't given them a couple of extra tickets, they never would have come. Your father wasn't at all interested in Shakespeare." At this point, her mother always leaned back and laughed out loud. Sometimes Beebe would join in—not interested in Shakespeare! Imagine, her own father not being interested in Shakespeare!

"But then, but then," said her mother, eyes shining, mouth smiling, "then, he said, when he saw me, he said I was the whole play . . . the best one . . . and it was true, Beebe. I was. Then, he said, then he got interested in Shakespeare . . . because of me."

Again her mother would laugh, and Beebe would laugh too. Those were the best times for both of them—talking about the past when Beebe's mother had been a young, lovely actress and Beebe's father had fallen in love with her.

"So there I was, eating breakfast all alone in one of those dinky diners, and up comes this guy—a sweet, little guy—and he says, 'Pardon me, Miss, but weren't you in the play last night?'

" 'Yes,' I say to him, 'Yes, I was.'

" 'You were wonderful,' he says. 'I never saw anybody act like you. But I don't want to interrupt you. I just wanted to tell you I thought you were wonderful. I'll never forget you.' "

Beebe's mother's face sometimes when she got to this point looked so young and happy that Beebe wanted her to stop talking. To just stop and remember that perfect time when nothing was wrong.

Because afterwards everything went wrong. Not right away because they married within the year, and, even though Beebe's mother got pregnant, she and Beebe's father agreed that wouldn't stop her from acting. Nothing would stop her.

But something did. Beebe's father developed leukemia. That stopped her. And when he died there was no money, and a full-time job to contend with, and Beebe to take care of, and Beebe's career as an actress to develop.

Beebe waited, leaning against the door, for the bitter words her mother would speak next, and prepared to counter with soft, soothing words of her own. She watched the tension in her mother's face, saw the taut lines of her lips as they stretched across her teeth—it was all so familiar—and now those harsh words would issue forth. . . .

Suddenly, surprisingly, Beebe's mother's face changed. Her mouth softened, her eyes opened, and she said—she actually said—"Well, never mind, Beebe. It's not the end of the world."

Beebe crumpled up against the door. "Wh-what?" she asked.

Her mother smiled. "I said it's not the end of the world, Beebe. You did the best you could. I know you did. I heard you—you were marvelous. But if you're going to be an actress, you're just going to have to get used to a certain amount of rejection. You have to be a little tougher skinned." She cocked her head to one side, and inspected Beebe as she clung to the door. "You take things much too hard, honey. You really do. I keep telling you not to make such a big deal of it."

Beebe burst out crying. She was sixteen years old, and for at least eight years now, she had never been able to cry over all those years of rejection. Her mother had cornered the market on suffering until now, for the first time, Beebe was able to play the leading role.

It was wonderful. She wept. She raged. She screamed at her mother that Jennifer Evans, who got the part of Juliet, was a big, stupid girl with a loud voice who made Juliet sound like a yodeler. She cried that Mrs. Kronberger hadn't even let her finish reading the part, had been distracted, and hadn't really listened. That it wasn't fair. That she hadn't had a real chance. That none of it was fair, that it never was.

Somewhere along the line, she had been gathered up into her mother's arms, and it was all so lovely having her mother rock her and croon soft, soothing words in her ear. ". . . next time . . . never mind . . . it's not so important. . . ."

Beebe did not want to waste the opportunity. She attacked each person who had gotten a major role (except for Dave Mitchell/Romeo) and then went on to complain about the lousy acoustics and the noisy seats. Her mother continued rocking and crooning, so Beebe moved on to all the other painful areas in her life. There were years of hurts, slights, and failures to lament—how much her new contacts irritated her eyes, the B+ on her book report in English—a host of possibilities crowded into her head, clamoring to be heard, and Beebe had just taken a deep, satisfying breath before continuing when her mother said quickly, pushing her away slightly and smiling down into her face, "I know what. Let's go out to dinner."

"I can't," Beebe wailed. "I have to go to the library and get started on that dumb report for history. I haven't got time to eat."

Which wasn't true, as her mother pointed out. "We'll have a quick bite, and then I'll drive you over to the library and get some books out for myself at the same time. You can pick the restaurant."

The food was so good at the new Thai restaurant, and Beebe was so hungry, that it wasn't until she had gobbled down the curried chicken and most of the Pad-Thai that she realized her mother was hardly eating anything.

"What's wrong, Mom?" Beebe said nervously. "You're not eating anything."

Not that Beebe's mother was such a big eater at any time. Both Beebe and her mother were small and slim, but usually it was Beebe's mother who had to urge Beebe to eat and not the other way around.

"Oh, nothing's the matter," her mother said, poking the food on her plate with her chopsticks but not raising any of it to her lips. She smiled at Beebe, and her pretty face quivered with excitement. "Everything's fine—really fine. The sale ended today."

"Oh?" Beebe examined her mother's face questioningly. Something had to be responsible for that heightened glow. "Did you buy yourself any shoes?"

Her mother worked as an assistant sales manager in a very expensive shoe store. Most of the shoes came from France or Italy, and generally her mother spoke bitterly of the wealthy women who could afford to buy three or four pairs of shoes at a time, shoes that sold for hundreds of dollars a single pair. Beebe's mother had beautiful, slim legs and graceful, high-arched feet, but it was only after a sale that the staff was allowed to buy the dregs and leftovers, the mismatched shoes, the ones with scuffs and flaws.

"No, I didn't buy anything," her mother said cheerfully. "That dental bill last month was a killer, and you're going to need a new jacket."

Beebe picked up some of the noodles with her chopsticks, and carried them to her mouth. She savored their clear, sharp, sweet taste and chewed slowly. It didn't seem to her that the dental bill or the new jacket should be making her mother so happy.

Her mother laughed out loud and pushed the food around some more. "But I really did enjoy the day. It was a . . . fun day."

"Oh?" Beebe swallowed a mouthful of noodles, and waited.

"We were busy, busy, busy from the moment I opened the store until we closed. And Florence Sadler didn't show up again. That woman is impossible. No call. No nothing. As far as I'm concerned, she's finished. So the rest of us had to kill ourselves taking care of the customers, and I couldn't even stop for lunch."

This was a much more familiar conversation, except for her mother's cheerful recounting of it.

"And then, at just about three in the afternoon, when I was trying to help a bunch of customers at the same time, Melissa asked me to deal with this man who wanted to return a pair of Maud Frizon shoes bought on sale yesterday. I explained to him that the sale was final, and that we never give refunds for this kind of special sale but would be willing to let him have a credit. No! He said no! He wanted the money. He really became almost unpleasant." Beebe's mother was smiling now.

"But you're used to people like that," Beebe said. "Aren't most of your customers unpleasant?"

"Oh, yes," said her mother, nodding. "Oh, yes. But then most of them are rich, older women. And this man—well, he must be around my age, nice looking, tall, red-headed—not dressed in business clothes, not anybody who works on Montgomery Street, that's for sure."

Now Beebe was finished. She laid her chopsticks on her plate and waited.

Her mother also laid her chopsticks down. "He said his sister bought the shoes, and that she was home with a sick kid and asked him to return them for her. He said she really needed the money, and I kept right on explaining the store's policy. So after a while, he calmed down. I told him again, as pleasantly as I could, that we would be happy to give him a credit, but he said no." Beebe's mother shook her head and smiled. "He said he would come back tomorrow and continue the argument. He asked me to have lunch with him, and I said . . ."

"Yes," Beebe finished the sentence.

"No! I said no." Her mother's cheeks grew pink. "But I guess I didn't say it very strongly, because he said he would be back tomorrow around noon, and he hoped I would change my mind."

"I have to go to the library," Beebe said, standing up. "That report is due in a few days, and I have to get started."

Her mother dropped her in front of the library. "I'll park," she said, "and meet you inside."

As Beebe hurried up the stairs, she thought nervously about her mother. It was seldom that her mother ever went out with men. Once in a while, some friend would come up with a divorced brother or a neighbor with a widowed son. Nobody her mother had ever liked especially. She hardly ever met any men at the store. It surprised Beebe to see her mother so animated. Of course, she had no objection to her mother meeting some nice man—eventually. At least, she didn't think she had any objection.

Somebody at the top of the stairs held the door open for her, and she murmured "Thanks!" as she passed inside.

The girl was moving so quickly that Mark had to press up against the door or she would have knocked the books out of his hands. "Thanks!" she said as she whizzed by, and he looked angrily at her little, skinny back and restrained himself from yelling after her, "Why don't you watch where you're going?"

He carried his books down the stairs, crossed the street, turned the corner, and stopped. Carelessly—he tried to make it seem carelessly—and slowly, he pulled the car keys out of his pocket before inserting them into the lock. Dope, he said to himself, you're on the wrong side. He smiled foolishly at a woman who was stepping out of the car in front of his, but she was busy locking her car—one of those little subcompacts—and didn't notice him.

He still wasn't used to driving around by himself. He'd only moved in with his father five days ago, and this was the third time his father had simply tossed the car keys to him and told him to take the van. No fuss, no worry, no nervous questions.

He walked around to the driver's side, opened the door, and slid inside. His hand trembled as he put the key into the ignition, and he sat still for a moment, savoring the surge of power that swelled up inside of him.

Why had he waited so long to move in with his father? Why? His mother's teary face appeared inside his mind, and he tried to ignore it. She still had Marcy and Jed to look after. And it wasn't as if he were going off to Tibet. He'd call her, and go over on Sundays sometimes. She knew he'd never neglect her.

He started the engine, and listened to it growl. He liked the van—it made him feel manly to drive something so big and rugged. His mother drove a little Chevy Nova, and she fussed over it and babied it and coddled it as if it were another kid. She hardly ever let him drive it alone—not without a bunch of instructions and restrictions and arguments. She still treated him as if he were twelve years old like Marcy, and not sixteen and a half. She didn't like him driving at all, and kept showing him all the latest figures on teenage deaths on the highway. He smiled grimly, remembering how she had refused at first even to sign the permission form for him to get a permit. Now he could smile, but then, when he was fifteen and a half, he hadn't smiled. He had simply decided that maybe he would be happier living with his father.

He put the van in reverse, and backed up a few inches. That woman who had parked in front of him hadn't left him much room. He tapped her bumper on his first attempt to pull out. Nothing serious but the car shuddered. It was only a little subcompact. He backed up again, and then pulled out easily.

His father had always said he could come and stay with him anytime he wanted. Ever since the divorce seven years ago his father kept repeating that he would be welcome anytime he was ready to make the move.

Mark stopped for a light, opened his window, and leaned one elbow on it. Of course, when Mark first suggested it his mother had said no way! She said his father was irresponsible, undependable, selfish, and didn't mean what he said anyway. "That man never changed a diaper or fed a bottle to a baby in his life," she kept saying. Well, Mark didn't need a diaper changed anymore, and he didn't drink out of bottles either, but it had taken over a year before she had finally agreed. "You'll be back," she told him. He knew he would not.

His father's apartment—his now, too—was only a mile or so from the library, and he didn't want to stop driving. So he passed the street where they lived, and headed out towards the ocean. His father wouldn't mind if he stayed out a little longer. His mother, on the other hand, would start fussing if he was fifteen minutes late.

He turned onto the Great Highway, and increased his speed. It was cool, and the ocean breezes rippled across his head. A new life for him, that's what it was. A new life in a big, magic city. He'd felt confined out in San Leandro. It was foggy up ahead, and he frowned. Fog. That was the only part of living in San Francisco he wasn't going to like. There was too much fog. The last few nights had been so foggy that he hadn't been able to see much through his telescope.

But his father had insisted that the winter skies were usually clear. Mark also knew that there was an amateur astronomer's group here in the city that held monthly meetings and had star parties up at Mount Tam. He would get in touch with them in the next day or so. Back in San Leandro, aside from Mr. Benson at school, he hadn't found anybody who was really interested in astronomy.

At Sloat Boulevard, Mark reluctantly turned and began heading back to his father's—no—back home. It was his home now. Sure, some things seemed a little strange, but he would get used to them. His room was tiny, hardly more than a closet, and the place was pretty sloppy, and—this was kind of embarrassing but he was sixteen and a half—he knew he was interfering with his father's love life.

He stopped at a stop sign, and two women hesitantly swayed on the curb, watching him. Magnanimously, he motioned for them to cross, and they smiled and nodded at him as they passed. He smiled back, and kept smiling once he started driving again. His father would probably let him drive almost any time he wanted. Probably even on the Sundays when he visited his mother out in San Leandro, he guessed his father would simply toss him the keys and let him take the van. Wouldn't she be surprised when he pulled up in it? She'd probably say his father was just being irresponsible to let him drive it. Well, it didn't really matter what she said anymore. All he'd have to say was that it was okay with Dad.

This Saturday he would start working in his father's hardware store, and he would continue to work there every Saturday, and a couple of afternoons during the week as well. Maybe his father would need him to run errands with the van—make deliveries, pick up stuff. He'd do whatever his father asked him to do. He liked the idea of working in the store.

Mark turned off the avenue and onto his father's— his street. No problem parking—there were two spots up near the corner. He backed into the smaller one just for the practice. The van handled like a dream. He turned off the motor, pulled up the emergency brake, and patted the dashboard lovingly. He should have moved in with his father years ago.

His father was sitting in front of the TV, watching Monday night football, when he came in.

"Close game," he said, smiling up at Mark. "They sacked Montana four times—but nothing can stop him."

"Oh, yeah?" Mark laughed uncomfortably. He hated football, but fortunately his father didn't seem to know it. His father proceeded to give him some of the details of the game, and he tried to look interested.

"I guess it's too late to go out for the team?" his father said.

"Uh—what?" Mark asked.

"At school, I mean. I guess they've held all the tryouts already for the football team."

"Oh, right!" Mark agreed quickly. Then he added, "You know, Dad, I'm not really much into football."

"You've got the build," his father said approvingly. "If I'd had a pair of shoulders like yours I could have been a first-string player in school instead of sitting on the bench most of the time."

Mark shifted around under his father's scrutiny and tried to change the subject. "The library's pretty good here," he said. "They have a whole bunch of books on astronomy I've never seen before."

"Great! Great!" said his father, nodding at him and smiling. "Oh, I was also going to say I could take you to the game this Sunday. I've got an extra ticket."

"I thought you and Lauren were going. I thought you said all the tickets were sold out, and you only had two."

His father grinned foolishly. "It's all over with Lauren. That's why I've got the extra ticket."

"But Dad . . ." Mark began. He wanted to tell his father that he hoped it wasn't because of him. He had a feeling that maybe Lauren used to stay over, before he moved in with his father, and he wanted to say that he was sixteen and a half, not a baby anymore, and that he understood all these matters. No sweat, he wanted to tell his father. He understood, and it was okay, and he wanted his father to know that he wasn't a prude, and that he'd feel lousy if his father had broken up with Lauren because of him.

Not that he liked Lauren especially. Not that he liked her at all, as a matter of fact. She was kind of a silly, over–made-up woman, who laughed a lot and looked at him in a bold, scary way.

"No, no," his father said. "It didn't have anything to do with you. I know that's what you're thinking, and it just isn't so. Besides, you're old enough to understand. You've probably even got a girl of your own."

"No!" Mark felt his ears growing warm. "No. I mean . . . not now."

His father nodded. "You'll meet plenty of nice girls at school. A guy with your looks won't ever have any trouble. But anyway, about Lauren, I've been getting tired of her. She spends money like it was water. The last straw was her birthday. I asked her what she wanted and she said a pair of shoes. So I told her to buy herself a pair, and I'd reimburse her. I figured fifty, sixty dollars—okay, maybe a hundred tops. So she went and bought herself a pair of fancy French shoes. She paid two hundred and fifty dollars for them. And they were on sale. That did it!"

"Two hundred and fifty dollars?" Mark repeated in horror.

"I'm not kidding," his father said grimly. "That was the last straw."

"I could buy a new telescope mount with two hundred and fifty dollars," Mark said.

"That's right," his father said. "I told her if it was for something worthwhile—for a tape deck or something important—but just for a lousy pair of shoes. Wait, I'll show them to you."

His father jumped up and hurried out of the room. When he returned he was holding up a red snakeskin, high-heeled sandal with one hand, and cradling a shoe box with the other.

"Here—just look at what she paid two hundred and fifty dollars for, on sale."

He held the sandal out to Mark, who picked it up by one thin strap and held it out, away from him, as if it were something unclean. Mark shook his head and murmured, "Mom never wears shoes like this."

"Crazy," his father said. "Absolutely crazy."

"But Dad," Mark said, handing the shoe back to his father, "why do you have the shoes and not Lauren?"

"Because," said his father, carefully parting the tissue paper that lined the inside of the box and settling the shoe into it, "I let her know what I thought. I mean I gave her the money—I did say she could buy whatever she liked—but I also let her know what I thought of somebody who would go out and spend two hundred and fifty dollars for a stupid pair of shoes. She said I was cheap and I said—well, it doesn't matter what I said, but she gave me the shoes. Actually, she threw them at me. Thank God she didn't damage them. I want my money back."

"Oh," said Mark, "are you going to take them back to the store?"

His father put the box down carefully and closed the lid. "I did already but they don't want to give me a refund." He smiled at Mark. "But you know your dad, Mark. He doesn't take no for an answer. I'm going back tomorrow, and you can be sure I'm going to end up with that refund."

Mark smiled back. "Do you want me to go along?"

"No, no, son, that's all right," his father said. "But I will take you to the Forty-niners game this Sunday. Don't forget. We have a date."

Mark retreated to his room, opened the window, and looked up at the sky. Although it was too foggy for him to see anything at all, he knew that tonight the lovely Corona Borealis would be shining in the western sky, the Big Dipper in the north, and Orion over in the east. The thin row of stars in Orion's belt made him think of the thin strap on that ridiculous red high-heeled shoe.

He rested his head on one hand, and thought about the shoe. No girl he'd ever care about would wear a shoe like that. No! The girl he'd care about would have to be a real person—interested in astronomy or something serious. Not one of those silly, giggly girls. She'd be a no-nonsense person, somebody you could talk to. She wouldn't wear a lot of makeup or dumb high-heeled shoes.

Not the girl he'd like. The girl he'd like would have to be somebody you could talk to, smart, serious, and interesting. She wouldn't be giggling all the time, and looking at him with that bold, embarrassing look Lauren had. And she certainly would never wear high-heeled, expensive French shoes.

Mark hadn't met her yet, but he knew she wouldn't.

Beebe bent over and tied the shoelaces on one of her running shoes. Then she leaned back in her seat in the back of the auditorium and listened. Dave Mitchell/Romeo was rehearsing up on the stage with Todd Merster/Benvolio. He was saying:

> "Love is a smoke made with the fume of sighs;
> Being purg'd, a fire sparkling in lovers' eyes;
> Being vex'd, a sea nourish'd with lovers' tears:
> What is it else? a madness most discreet,
> A choking gall, and a preserving sweet."

Her lips moved along with the words, but Dave was saying them too quickly and finished before she did.

"Slow down," Mrs. Kronberger said to him. "Try it again."

This time Beebe whispered them along with him out loud. There was nobody else sitting in the back of the auditorium to hear her. As far as she was concerned, this was the most beautiful passage in the whole play because it described so well how she felt about Dave Mitchell.

"A madness most discreet"—that's exactly what it was, because it was almost more than she could bear and yet nobody knew how she felt about him. Not her mother, not Wanda, certainly not Dave Mitchell.

"A choking gall." Yes, that too, because so many times when she met him in the hall, or saw him in class, or even here at rehearsal, so many times, when she'd practiced some cute or funny or charming words—they could never rise out of her throat. They died there while she only managed to choke out something inane and colorless.

"A preserving sweet." Yes, her feeling for Dave was a preserving sweet. Her daydreams about him had gone on and on for nearly a year now. They were preserved, and they were very, very sweet.

"Romeo's shallow," her mother said. "He's a typical, macho teenager. At the beginning of the play, he's madly in love with Rosaline. Then he goes to a dance, sees Juliet, and in a few seconds, is even more madly in love with her, just because she's prettier. He's got no character. But Benedick . . ."

Beebe didn't want to hear about Benedick. It was bad enough that her mother had insisted on naming her Beatrice—her father had preferred Miranda from *The Tempest,* a much prettier name as far as Beebe was concerned—but the two lovers in *Much Ado About Nothing* just yacked and yacked like middle-aged adults. They lacked the passion and ferocity of the lovers in *Romeo and Juliet.*

"People change," Beebe always said, defending Romeo. "You said you liked somebody in your acting company until you met Dad."

"Yes, but I fell in love with Dad because of what he was, not for what he looked like. Ted Ritter, the guy in my company, was very good-looking, but he was kind of shallow too, just like Romeo."

"People change," Beebe repeated stubbornly. And maybe Dave would change too. Right now, he and Jennifer Evans/Juliet were going around together. They'd been together since last year when both of them had gotten the leading roles in *Twelfth Night.*

Now they were both up on stage, rehearsing scene 5, the big one where Romeo sees Juliet for the first time. Beebe clenched her fists, and whispered the words along with Dave:

> "What lady is that which doth enrich the hand
> Of yonder knight?"

"Don't mumble," Mrs. Kronberger said, "and remember to keep your chin up. We're losing half the words out here."

Dave nodded and smiled good-naturedly at her. Beebe's heart beat faster. How good-looking he was with his short, curly brown hair, his large, dark eyes, his slim, graceful figure. And how nice he was—for such a boy, such a star. He wasn't at all conceited or mean-spirited. Just the other day when she met him in the hall, and dropped her notebook and all the papers had gone flying, he'd helped her pick everything up, laughing and making her feel almost good about dropping it, almost as if she'd finally done something right, something to get his attention and approval.

His voice wasn't really projecting well, but there were a couple of kids horsing around over on the left side of the auditorium. She shot them a ferocious look as Romeo mumbled:

"O! she doth teach the torches to burn bright.
It seems she hangs upon the cheek of night
Like a rich jewel in an Ethiop's ear;"

"Louder and slower, louder and slower," Mrs. Kronberger repeated. "And get a little more feeling into it. You're not reading a shopping list."

"Beauty too rich for use, for earth too dear!"

Jennifer Evans/Juliet walked over to the front of the stage and called out, "Mrs. Kronberger, I'm going to have to go in fifteen minutes."

"I know, I know," said the teacher. "You have to go to the dentist. I know."

"Well, can we just move ahead to my part?"

"We purposely moved on ahead to scene five and skipped the first scene so we could accommodate you," Mrs. Kronberger said crankily. "I thought your appointment was at four-thirty."

"No, it's at four," Jennifer said gently.

"I don't know why there's always a bunch of people

who have to go to the dentist during rehearsals," Mrs. Kronberger said even more crankily. "What is it with this generation anyway? I never went to the dentist when I was your age."

"So would it be okay to do the end of the scene now?" Jennifer coaxed. "I'll try to make my appointments later from now on."

"No, it's not okay," Mrs. Kronberger said savagely. "I just don't want to rush through this scene. Especially since everybody else is here for a change. Where is your understudy?"

Beebe stood up immediately. Her legs were trembling, but she stood up. It was going to happen, finally. Now. She was going to stand up there on the stage with Dave, and hold the part in front of her, and pretend to read the lines that she already knew by heart:

"Good pilgrim, you do wrong your hand too much,
Which mannerly devotion shows in this;
For saints have hands that pilgrims' hands do touch,
And palm to palm is holy palmers' kiss."

And he would take her hand, and he would pull her close to him, and after a while, he would say:

"Then move not, while my prayers' effect I take.
Thus from my lips, by thine, my sin is purg'd."

And then he would kiss her, and she would . . .

"I really will try, Mrs. Kronberger, to make my appointments later. Honestly, I will. And you know this is only the first time it's happened," Jennifer said.

Mrs. Kronberger mumbled something and waved a hand impatiently. But then she told the others to sit down while Romeo and Juliet went into their big introduction scene.

Beebe sat down too. She was bitterly disappointed but relieved at the same time. She watched as Jennifer and Dave moved together to the center of the stage. Mrs. Kronberger started to cough, and while she was coughing, the two leading players turned towards each other smiling. Beebe jealously saw how Dave leaned over and put an arm around Jennifer's shoulder as he whispered something to her. Jennifer moved into the circle of his arm, and settled comfortably against him.

There was a deep sorrow inside of Beebe as she watched the two of them together—Dave with his handsome, bright, humorous face so close to Jennifer's long blonde hair. And Jennifer looking up at him, out of her large blue eyes. She was such a pretty girl it hurt Beebe. Such a pretty girl and, yes, such a nice girl too.

Why did she have to be so pretty and so nice? It wasn't fair that some people had everything. No wonder they always got the leading parts.

Mrs. Kronberger stopped coughing. "Well, if you two can separate yourselves and concentrate on the play . . ." she said, trying to sound severe but not really succeeding. How could anybody be severe with Dave and Jennifer? ". . . perhaps we can begin."

Beebe leaned forward and listened. The day she had had the crying jag she had said, spitefully, to her mother that Jennifer was a big, stupid girl with a loud voice like a yodeler. As Jennifer read her lines, Beebe knew it wasn't true. Jennifer was lovely, and not stupid at all. Her voice was rich and clear, and she spoke her lines with a sweetness and a playfulness that penetrated Beebe's sorrow and made her want to clap her hands. She knew, without wanting to admit it, that Jennifer was much more talented than Dave. When Jennifer spoke her lines Beebe felt as if she were hearing them for the first time.

"My only love sprung from my only hate!
Too early seen unknown, and known too late!
Prodigious birth of love it is to me,
That I must love a loathed enemy."

Yes, yes, Beebe thought, wrapped up as she was in her knotted feelings for Jennifer. She was—she should be—a loathed enemy because Dave liked her, but yet Beebe couldn't hate Jennifer just as Juliet couldn't hate Romeo.

It was all so complicated. There were times nothing made sense at all. If Dave hadn't taken care of Mr. Ferguson when he had that epileptic seizure down in the lunchroom last year, she probably never would have developed a crush on him. Oh yes, she probably would have admired him in the drama group, but the memory of him, leaning over the purple-faced, foaming Mr. Ferguson, loosening his collar and gently turning his head to one side . . . Dave's bright, handsome face so kind and competent. If she hadn't been down in the lunchroom that day, a warm, clear, lovely October day . . . She had even brought a sandwich to school and planned on eating it outside with Wanda, and just because Wanda asked Leslie Cooper, who laughed all the time, to join them, she changed her mind. She couldn't stand people who laughed all the time over nothing. So she didn't go with them. She said she was in a hurry, and she went down to the lunchroom, and there he was, as she entered, surrounded by a circle of bit players, and poor Mr. Ferguson foaming and purple-faced lying on the ground and Dave occupying center stage. Ever since then, he had occupied center stage in her daydreams.

"Okay, okay, not bad," Mrs. Kronberger said. "Now, scram—you Jennifer, only you! And let's all take a few minutes' break, and start up from the beginning. I want all the kids in act one, scene one, to take their places up on the stage. I'll be back in a few minutes."

Beebe rose and began moving towards the stage. If she had eaten her sandwich outside with Wanda and Leslie, or if he hadn't been in the lunchroom just at that moment when Mr. Ferguson had his seizure . . . so many ifs.

The cast was assembling on the stage—the two Capulet servants, the one Montague servant, Benvolio, Tybalt, assorted citizens, police, Capulet and Lady Capulet, Montague and herself, Lady Montague (with only two speaking parts—even Lady Capulet had more than that), the Prince, and, finally, Romeo.

He was clowning around on the stage with some of the other boys. A few of them were whirling their wooden swords around, and Dave dove across the stage, chasing Fred Gee/Tybalt and nearly bumping into her.

"Oops," he said, steadying himself by putting a hand on her arm.

She laughed nervously.

Dave's face was pink, and his eyes shone. "I nearly knocked over my mother." He bowed to her. "Forgive me, my dear Mother," he said, already focusing on Tybalt, who was jabbing him with his sword, "while I go take care of this cursed Capulet."

This was one of those times that Beebe should have been ready with some funny or charming words that would attract his attention.

"Oh, that's okay," she said, and watched as he chased Tybalt across the stage.

His father handed him a broom. "The first thing," he said, "is to sweep out the toilet. Every new worker gets broken in that way."

Joe and Kelly, the two part-time college boys who worked for his father on Saturdays, laughed, and Kelly said, "That's why I'm so glad you're low man on the totem pole, Mark. Now I'm off the hook."

Mark smiled and tried to look pleased. Not that he liked the idea of sweeping out the toilet. But he didn't dislike it either. And he liked having his father treat him just like any other of his workers.

He took the broom, and went off to the back of the store. The floor of the toilet looked pretty clean to him, but he started sweeping anyway. His father came and stood at the door. 'That's the first thing I had to do when I came to work here. The boss, Mr. Altobelli, he said to me, 'You've got to sweep your way out of the toilet before you learn anything else.' "

"That's okay, Dad," Mark said, moving the broom behind the door to show his father he intended to be thorough.

"Attaboy," said his father, patting him on the back. "We're going to have a great time together—you and I."

"Sure thing, Dad," Mark said, trying to sound enthusiastic. And he did feel enthusiastic, he thought, pushing the broom behind the toilet. There wasn't much room there, but he poked at it with the corner of the broom and managed to dislodge a clump of dust.

"Garden hoses?" he heard his father say behind him. "You passed them on your way in. Come with me, and I'll show you where they are."

Mark finished sweeping, and then began wandering around the store. His father had told him to start learning where everything was. *Paints and painting supplies over on the left-hand side in front of the electrical supplies. Housewares in the front. Plumbing supplies in the back. Pipe threader in the center . . .*

"Mark," his father called out, "will you give Kelly a hand carrying out the cans?"

He and Kelly carried some green plastic trash cans outside the store, and then Kelly showed him where he should display them. "We need to bring out the galvanized cans, too, some garden chairs, and the carpet-cleaning machine."

But then Joe had to go deliver some paints, and

Mark's father called Kelly inside to make a set of keys for a customer. So Mark carried out the other trash cans, the garden chairs, and the cleaning machine by himself. He wasn't sure whether the cleaning machine was supposed to go next to the trash cans or on the other side of the garden chairs. Kelly hadn't said, and he felt foolish about asking. He wandered back into the store and waited for further orders. Kelly was busy at the key machine making up some duplicates for an older woman. She was telling him why she needed extra keys, and he was trying to look interested.

". . . so my son thinks maybe he'll stay with me now for a couple of months until he finds a job. I don't mind. It's nice to have the company. But then he tells me this morning that a friend of his is coming down from Portland who wants to be an actress. A girl, you see. He says she's just a friend, but he wants me to have a whole set of keys made up for her. I said to him, 'Why don't you have them made up. She's your friend. I'm your mother, not your slave.' So then he says . . ."

Mark's father was in the back, showing window shades to another customer. Mark began walking up and down the aisles again, trying to memorize where things were. *Weather stripping, water heater blankets, nuts and bolts . . .* His father, carrying a couple of shades and followed by the customer, smiled at him and headed towards the front of the store. "Just look around, Mark, and later I'll show you how to work the cash register. As soon as things quiet down."

It took a while before they did. Mark kept wandering up and down the aisles. *Towel racks, two-by-fours, power tools* . . . He never realized one small hardware store would carry so many different items. *Doorknobs, paintbrushes, light bulbs* . . . Well, right now it seemed overwhelming but his memory was excellent. Didn't he know all the principal constellations and all of the important stars in the solar system? Probably, in a few weeks, he'd know where everything was in the store.

Wire, locks, hand tools, pot holders . . . You had to be patient, and soon everything would fall into place. School, for instance. It had taken him nearly a week to find his way around. All of his classes seemed to be so far apart, and there were so many kids, and he didn't know a single one of them. *Saws, ant killer, window sprays* . . . A hard tug of homesickness rocked him, and he put out an arm to steady himself against a shelf of cookie tins. He thought of Gilbert Jennings and Jim Turner. He'd never thought of them as close friends, but now he missed them. And he thought of Cindy Rhinehart.

He and Cindy had been friends for a couple of years. They used to spend a lot of time together. Once he'd even gone backpacking with Cindy and her family, and a couple of times she'd slept over at his house (in Marcy's room) when they studied math together. She was a real math whiz, and whenever he needed any help she was always there.

He liked Cindy, and he knew she liked him. But nothing else ever happened. They walked a lot together. They talked and listened to one another. But nothing romantic ever happened. Maybe if he'd stayed in San Leandro their feelings for each other would have changed. She was exactly the kind of girl he liked—he should have liked—smart, serious, and pretty, too, in a careless way. But, of course, he thought quickly, it didn't really matter what she looked like.

Doormats, spot removers, wire shelves . . .

"You're Mark Driscoll, aren't you?" the girl said.

She was standing in the aisle, just in front of him, as he came towards her.

"Uh—yes." She was tall with long blonde hair and big blue eyes. He recognized her from one of his classes.

"What are you doing here?" she asked, smiling at him in a friendly, comfortable way. His homesickness began to fade.

"I work here," he told her. "I mean, I just started today. This is my father's store."

"No kidding!" she said. "I've been coming here for years. I live right around the corner, but I never saw you here before."

"Well . . ." Mark began, and smiled. He guessed he would have to tell her that his parents were divorced, and he'd been living with his mother, but now he was with his father, and maybe he and she could . . .

A guy came around the aisle. "Oh, there you are, Jenny. Did you find the lighter fluid?" He put an arm around the girl's shoulder, and she said to Mark, "This is my boyfriend, Dave Mitchell. Dave, this is Mark Driscoll. He's in my Spanish class, and in my English class too."

"How you doin', Mark?" Dave held out a hand, and Mark took it and gave it a quick shake.

"We're having a cookout at my house tonight," Jennifer said. "The weather turned so warm we suddenly decided to invite a bunch of our friends over, and just stuff our faces."

"Oh, that sounds great," Mark said, feeling left out and trying hard not to show it.

"Why don't you come too?" Jennifer added. "We could use a few more guys."

"Well . . . I don't know. I have to work until six."

"His father owns the store," Jennifer explained to Dave.

"No kidding," Dave said. "I come in here lots of times but I've never seen you here before."

He was going to have to explain. Both of them were looking at him—smiling and waiting.

"My parents are divorced," he said. "I've been living with my mother, but now I'm living with my dad."

"So that's why we've never seen you around," Jennifer said. "Well, you come after work. You'll meet a whole bunch of nice kids. There's Robin Vargas and Todd Merster and Carole Yin and Frank Jackson. . . . Do you know any of them?"

"I think Todd Merster is in my P.E. class."

"He's a kick," Jennifer said, "and the girls are nice too. I should tell you that most of them are in the Drama Club. They'll be in the school play next spring. Are you interested in acting? We need a few more guys."

"No," Mark said quickly, "I'm not interested in acting. I never was."

"Well, never mind," Jennifer said. "You'll like the kids. Some of the girls are really cool."

"I'll say," Dave laughed, and rolled his eyes around. Jennifer bumped him with her hip. He bumped her with his, and the two of them began tussling. Mark tried to look away. *Floor wax, mops, broom handles . . .*

Finally, Jennifer began talking again, a little breathlessly. "Wanda Bedrosian is coming—she's Lady Capulet in the play, and Rebecca Chin—she's a lot of fun—and Mollie George and . . ."

"And that cute, little, dark girl with the big eyes. What's her name? She plays my mother in the play," Dave said. "Did you ask her?"

"Beebe Clarke—that's right. She's coming, and Dorrie Ferguson. Do you know her?"

Mark didn't know any of the girls, but he said he'd try to come if his father didn't need him. Jennifer gave him her address, and he watched as she and Dave walked out of the store, hand in hand. Maybe he would call Cindy tonight just to see how she was. Hadn't she said to him before he left, "Keep in touch"?

Maybe if she was free, he could go home tomorrow, to his mother's, that is. But no, his father had tickets to a '49ers game, and he was going. Well, he could still give Cindy a ring tonight, just to see how she was. He could call her before he went to Jennifer's party—if he went to Jennifer's party. He didn't know any of the kids, and all of them were into acting anyway. He didn't think he'd have anything in common with a bunch of kids who liked to act.

Things began to quiet down in the store, and his father taught him how to use the cash register. He felt better once he learned the cash register, and, after a while, his father didn't have to hang around watching him ring up the sales. That was even better.

At two o'clock, his father said, "Come on, Mark, we'll go have some lunch."

Kelly took his place at the cash register, and Mark followed his father out of the store, up the block, and into a small coffee shop.

"Eat whatever you like, Mark," said his father. "You earned it today."

"I didn't do that much," Mark protested, but still he was pleased that his father approved of his work. They both ordered hamburgers, and while they waited for their order his father talked about his plans for Mark.

"Later, I'm going to have you unpack some of the electrical supplies, and maybe next week I'll teach you how to make keys. . . ."

Mark hoped his father would tell him he could do the deliveries, but his father went on to talk about mixing paint and threading pipe and didn't say anything about driving the van.

Their hamburgers arrived. They both began eating, and then his father said suddenly, "Oh, Mark, about tomorrow."

"Right, Dad," he said, trying to sound pleased. "It's the big Forty-niner game. I haven't forgotten."

"Well, listen, Mark. I know I promised to take you, and I know you're going to be disappointed, but, hey, it's a long season. I'll get tickets for another game."

Mark couldn't believe his good luck. "What happened?" he asked.

His father smiled foolishly. "I asked somebody else."

"Lauren?"

"No, no, not her. I told you I'm finished with her." His father shook his head emphatically. "This is somebody else, somebody in another league altogether." He took a bite of his hamburger and chewed it reflectively. Mark waited.

"Her name is Barbara—and she's . . . well, she's different. I mean, not in a bad way—just different for me." His father held the hamburger in his hand and looked at Mark, a puzzled expression on his face.

"Did you just meet her, Dad?" Mark asked, trying to help his father along, trying to show him that it was okay for him to go out and to talk about it with his son who was sixteen and a half.

His father nodded gratefully, and leaned forward. "You remember the pair of shoes I was trying to return to that fancy shoe store downtown? I told you about that, and about how they didn't want to give me my money back. Remember?"

"Oh, sure, Dad. The pair Lauren bought?"

"Right. Well, the first time I went there, I had to speak to the assistant manager of the store, and she kept saying no, I couldn't get my money back. Only a credit. You know me, Mark, I don't take no for an answer. I noticed she was kind of pretty even though she was sort of . . . well . . . uptight."

"Is she Barbara?"

"Yes, but wait! Let me tell you what happened." His father grinned, and took another bite of his hamburger. Mark watched as he chewed it. His father had red hair, just like his, and it curled over his forehead, making him look much younger than his age, forty-two. He was a good-looking man, with bright, eager green eyes and a smile that twisted up on one side. It was twisting up now as he laid down his hamburger and continued.

"I went back the next day, and tried to get her to have lunch with me. I figured what's twenty bucks when I'll get back two hundred and fifty. She said no. But she said it in kind of a sorry way, like she wished she could have said yes. But she still said no about the refund. So yesterday, I went down again. By now it was getting to be fun, and both Kelly and Joe were able to work in the store. So this time, I got all dressed up in a tie and a shirt, and just sort of ambled into her place around twenty to twelve. I could see she was happy to see me. She tried not to show it, but she came over, and she had a hard time not smiling. 'You certainly are persistent,' she said. 'And I tell you what— you don't have to take me out to lunch. I've decided to give you a refund before you spend a fortune on gasoline.' " His father grinned. "Real sharp, don't you think?"

"Oh, sure, Dad," Mark said.

"Well, I told her I *wanted* to take her out to lunch, and if she said no, I'd just keep coming back, and her conscience would bother her because I would spend a fortune on gasoline."

Now his father laughed, and Mark laughed along with him. He wondered what this new one was going to be like. He hoped she wouldn't be anything like Lauren.

"She picked the place. You know some of them down there are out of sight. But she picked a nice, quiet, reasonable kind of place. And I enjoyed myself. She's . . . she's . . . different. She's smart, and she's . . . educated . . . but she's not stuck up . . . and she . . . well, she's pretty but she hardly uses any makeup, and she was just wearing a plain blue dress—nothing fancy. She's kind of small—you know I usually like tall women, but this one's small and sort of delicate. I don't know. . . ."

His father still had that puzzled look on his face, and Mark said encouragingly, "So she's a Forty-niner fan too?"

"Oh, no," said his father. "She hates football."

"But isn't she the one you're taking to the game?"

"Yes," his father answered, grinning again, "and that's why this is all so . . . well, different and fun. She said she hated competitive sports, and I told her it's because she just doesn't understand. She said she loved going to the theater, and she's especially crazy about Shakespeare. I told her what I thought about Shakespeare, and she said it's because I don't understand. I tell you, Mark, this is a first for me. So we agreed—she'll come with me to the game, and then I have to go with her to see a Shakespeare play." His father shook his head. "I tell you, this lady is one of a kind."

"She sounds real nice, Dad," Mark said. "And to tell you the truth, I really don't like football games either."

His father didn't pay any attention to what he said. "She has a daughter," his father continued. "I think she goes to your school. Her name is Beatrice—Beatrice Clarke. Maybe you know her."

"No, Dad, I don't think so." Mark decided he'd call Cindy as soon as he got home from the store that night. If she was free tonight maybe he'd go back to San Leandro to see her, and then he could spend tomorrow with his mother. He guessed he'd have to take BART. His father was going to need the van tomorrow to go to the game.

Cindy wasn't at home, and neither was his mother. His father was watching TV, and he felt restless and just a little sorry for himself.

"Dad," he said, "could I borrow the van?"

"Sure," said his father, throwing him the keys. He didn't ask him where he was going, but Mark told him anyway. "This girl in my class is having a cookout tonight, and she asked me to come."

"Great, great!" his father said. "Have a good time."

His father didn't ask him where the girl lived, and didn't say anything about a curfew.

He arrived late at the party. A few kids, Jennifer told him, had already come and gone. Jennifer's house had a big deck and a backyard. It was the clearest night he'd seen so far since moving to the city. He tried to point out some of the constellations to a cute girl named Wanda, but she asked him what his astrological sign was and whether or not he believed in astrology.

"No," he said, "no, I don't. I think it's silly." He was sorry afterwards that he used the word *silly*. He didn't want to hurt her feelings. But she just shrugged her shoulders.

"Neither does my best friend, Beebe," she said. "Do you know her?"

"No," he said. "I don't."

"Too bad she had to leave early. She and her mother had tickets to the theater." Wanda waved to a couple of kids who had just come out on the deck. "Hey Frank, Robin, come on down here, and look at the stars with us. Anyway, she's always yammering about how dumb astrology is, and she's got this quote from Shakespeare. She's always quoting Shakespeare—but I can't remember what it is."

"What was that quote you had about how stupid astrology is?" Wanda asked Beebe on Monday.

"Quote?"

"Oh, you know, Beebe, you're always throwing it at me. It's from Shakespeare, and it says people are creeps because they're creeps, not because of their astrological signs."

"Oh, you mean the one from *Julius Caesar,* the one that goes 'The fault, dear Brutus, is not in our stars / But in ourselves that we are underlings.' "

"Right. That's the one."

"Why do you ask?"

Wanda smiled. "I met this really cute boy at Jennifer's cookout Saturday. Really cute. Kind of tall with red hair—very shy. His name is Mark Driscoll. Do you know him?"

"No."

"Well, he's a new kid. Just moved into the neighborhood. Anyway, he's a bug on the stars, but when I told him I was into astrology he reacted the same way you do. I think you'd like this guy. He's kind of serious, like you."

"I'm not interested," Beebe said.

Wanda looked at her meaningfully and laughed a low, teasing laugh.

"Why are you laughing at me like that?" Beebe asked.

"Oh . . . because I can guess why you're not interested. Why you haven't been interested in any guy for nearly a year. You can't fool me."

"I don't know what you're talking about," Beebe said stiffly.

"I know a quote too," Wanda said, "and it's sort of from Lincoln. It goes, 'You can fool some of the people all of the time, and all of the people some of the time, but you can't fool your old friend Wanda. Period.'"

"You're crazy." Beebe tried to laugh.

"Listen, Sweetie." Wanda draped an arm across Beebe's shoulder. "I've been watching you at rehearsals. I mean, I've had my suspicions. But I've been watching you whenever *he* appears. You turn all colors, and you drop things and stammer if the great god talks to you. Take my advice, Beebe, and f-o-r-g-e-t him. He's all sewed up."

"Does it show?" Beebe asked nervously. "Does anybody else know?"

"Probably," Wanda said cheerfully. "You've got a real advanced case. But every other girl in the school has a crush on him too. Why not? He's the cutest guy in the whole place. But Jennifer's got him completely wrapped up. So if I were you . . ."

"Oh Wanda," Beebe said, "he's so great!" It was such a relief telling her best friend. Why had she kept it such a secret?

"Yes, he is," Wanda agreed. "But he's taken. Now this new kid . . ."

"Did you hear him on Friday in the balcony scene?"

"Sure—all of us had to come on Friday. But I thought Jennifer was wonderful. Didn't you? She wants to go into acting professionally, and I think she's already a smash."

"She *was* good," Beebe agreed, "but I thought Dave was so . . . so . . ."

"Well, he looked good, and when he can project his voice and stop mumbling, he sounds okay too."

Beebe thought about Dave's lines in the balcony scene.

"See! how she leans her cheek upon her hand:
O! that I were a glove upon that hand,
That I might touch that cheek."

She'd been whispering those lines over and over to herself all through the weekend, and daydreaming that Dave was saying them about her. She was also day-dreaming about what could, what might, what never would in real life, happen to the two of them after he'd said those lines.

"Are you coming to rehearsal today?" Wanda asked. "This is my big scene with Juliet."

Wanda was Lady Capulet, Juliet's mother. She had a much larger part than Lady Montague, Romeo's mother. If Wanda hadn't been Beebe's best friend, Beebe could have hated her for landing a part, without hardly trying, that was so much better than her own.

"I'm not in the rehearsal today," Beebe said. "But I guess I'll come anyway."

"I'm sure it's because you don't want to miss me," Wanda said, and proceeded to tell Beebe about this boy in her geometry class who changed his seat three times, and was now sitting behind her and whispering funny things into the back of her head. She thought he was an Aquarius, but there was also Frank Jackson in the Drama Club who was a Libra. . . .

Dave spoke to Beebe in the auditorium. He actually paused on his way to the stage, grinned at her, and said, "Hi, Mom."

She laughed nervously and then, thinking it over after he had passed, realized that what she should have said was, "Hi, Son!" Well, maybe next time if he said, "Hi, Mom," she could say, "Hi, Son." He'd probably like that. He might even stop and talk to her for a while.

Mrs. Kronberger was not in the auditorium on Monday in her accustomed place, complaining, arguing, lecturing. Most of the kids horsed around on stage while they waited for her. Beebe looked up at the clock in surprise. She couldn't remember Mrs. Kronberger ever being late. Finally, a short, puffy woman hurried into the auditorium, and spoke to them in a breathless voice.

"Mrs. Kronberger . . . must catch my breath . . . office forgot to get somebody . . . Mrs. Kronberger had a heart attack . . . very sorry . . . had to go to the hospital . . . very sudden . . . won't be back for six weeks or more."

All movement on the stage stopped. Beebe stood up from her seat at the back of the auditorium and hurried to the front, close to the messenger who sank into a seat and caught her breath while the others looked at her in horror.

"Our play," Wanda was the first to cry. "What's going to happen to our play?"

A chorus of questions were directed towards the small, puffy woman, who held up a comforting hand. "It's okay," she said. "Don't worry. I'm going to fill in until Mrs. Kronberger can come back. I'm Ms. Drumm. This is my first term here, and I teach computer science and P.E. I'll be your faculty advisor until she's better. So don't worry about a thing."

She smiled at them all, turning her head to include the kids on either side and behind her.

"Is she . . . is she . . . all right?" Beebe asked.

"What's that, dear?"

"Mrs. Kronberger? Is she all right?"

"Oh, yes. She's resting very comfortably. Nowadays, they can really make them very comfortable. But, of course, these things do take time, and I think it would be a very nice gesture if you sent her a card, and let her know you're thinking of her."

"I'll get it," Beebe offered. Even though Mrs. Kronberger had never given her a decent part in any play Beebe had tried out for, she felt a real connection to the teacher. Both of them loved Shakespeare, and next year, when she would be a senior, she had been looking forward to taking Mrs. Kronberger's honors English class.

"Fine. That's settled then. You can bring the card in tomorrow, and everybody can sign it."

"I think we should send flowers," Dave said. "Beebe, why don't you collect some money from everybody, and send her some flowers?"

He had called her by her name for the first time. He had singled her out. He had trusted her above all others to buy flowers for poor, sick Mrs. Kronberger.

"Oh, yes," Beebe said ardently. "I'll do it. Right away. Today."

He smiled at her—such a warm, friendly, trusting smile—and handed her two dollars. A little bustle of activity followed as other kids handed her money too. Suddenly she was important, and it was Dave Mitchell who had made it all happen.

"Now then," Ms. Drumm said, leaning back in her seat, "what play is it that you're doing?"

"*Romeo and Juliet,*" Jennifer told her.

"*Romeo and Juliet?* Isn't that a little heavy for high school kids?"

"We always do Shakespeare here," Rebecca Chin explained, "because Mrs. Kronberger has kind of a reputation for doing Shakespeare. Last year, we did *Twelfth Night,* and the year before we did *Julius Caesar.* But that didn't have enough girls' parts so some of us had to be men."

"But *Romeo and Juliet?*" Ms. Drumm persisted. "That's kind of sad, isn't it? And long?"

"Mrs. Kronberger took out some of the speeches and shortened a few others," Jennifer said, "but it is a tragedy so it's supposed to be sad."

"Everybody dies, don't they?" Ms. Drumm asked. "I think I saw it once or maybe I had to read it in school. Doesn't everybody die?"

Nobody said anything for a moment, and then Beebe tried. "Not *everybody* dies," she said carefully. "Romeo and Juliet die, and so do Tybalt, Mercutio, and Paris. And Lady Montague dies, too, but . . ."

"That's a lot of people," Ms. Drumm said thoughtfully. "Does Mrs. Kronberger know that all those people die?"

"Mrs. Kronberger *picked* the play," Dave said, smiling. "It doesn't bother us. Most of us are juniors and seniors. We know what's going on in the real world, and it's a lot worse than what's happening in this play."

Ms. Drumm continued to appear thoughtful. Then she smiled, nodded, and said, "Well, let's not worry about it now. What was supposed to happen today?"

"We're rehearsing act three, scene six," Wanda told her. "That's the scene with Lady Capulet—that's me— Juliet, Romeo, the nurse, and Capulet. Mrs. Kronberger was going to cut a little more out of the nurse's long speech and . . ."

"She was going to cut some out of your speech too," Rebecca said. Rebecca was the nurse.

"Why don't we just get started, and let me hear what you've got so far," Ms. Drumm suggested. "I'll try to talk to Mrs. Kronberger in a few days, but in the meantime let's just rehearse it the way you've been rehearsing it."

After the rehearsal, Beebe stopped at the big florist's on Geary, and sent off a dozen red roses to Mrs. Kronberger with a small florist's card on which she wrote, "With love from the kids in Drama." Then she stopped at the stationery store and mulled over the get-well cards. She finally ended up with a blank Sierra Club card that showed a splendid sunrise over the Pacific Ocean. Inside she wrote:

Dear Mrs. Kronberger,

We're all thinking about you and hoping you're feeling better. Get well soon. We miss you!

Then she added a quote from *Romeo and Juliet:*

Sleep dwell upon thine eyes, peace in thy breast.

She would bring it to school the next day and have all the kids in Drama sign it. She felt uncertain about Ms. Drumm. It was fortunate that somebody was willing to act as faculty advisor until Mrs. Kronberger recovered, but she didn't like Ms. Drumm's obvious disapproval of *Romeo and Juliet* as a school play.

"She thinks it's too heavy for a school play," she told her mother that night.

"I suppose it is heavy," said her mother, looking at the two dresses that she had just finished pressing and had hung up on the kitchen door. One was a dark blue dress with white piping around the collar, sleeves, and belt. The other was a green floral Laura Ashley dress that she hardly ever wore.

"I like the green better," Beebe said, "but you never wear it. Anyway, I don't think Ms. Drumm knows anything about Shakespeare. It doesn't matter if *Romeo and Juliet* is tragic. What matters is that it's so beautiful."

"Most people don't understand Shakespeare," her mother agreed, holding the green dress in front of her and moving out to stand in front of the long mirror in the hall. "Is this too long?"

"No, it isn't too long," Beebe told her. "Especially if you wear it with boots. You never wear boots."

"They're too warm to wear a whole day," said her mother, frowning at herself in the mirror. "But I'm not sure I like the way I look in this. It's kind of young."

"You're not so old," Beebe said kindly. "Anyway, I bought a get-well card for Mrs. Kronberger, and I put that line of Romeo's in it from act two: 'Sleep dwell upon thine eyes, peace in thy breast.' And I said we missed her and hoped she would get well soon."

Now Beebe's mother had taken down the blue dress, and was holding that one up in front of the mirror. "I think I look better in this one."

Beebe shrugged. "It's kind of dull, but . . ."

"Well, I could wear that bright red scarf, and maybe my coral beads."

Beebe stopped thinking about *Romeo and Juliet* and Mrs. Kronberger, and focused on her mother. "Why are you making such a fuss?" she asked. "You generally don't anguish so much over what you're going to wear to work."

"This isn't for work," said her mother, and looked embarrassed. "This is for next Saturday when I . . . when I go out with Jim."

"Oh, that's right," Beebe said. "You're taking him to see *Measure for Measure.*"

She and her mother had already seen the play on Saturday night, but they often saw the same Shakespeare play over again.

Beebe's mother shook her head, and turned to look at Beebe. "I wish they were doing *A Midsummer Night's Dream* or *The Taming of the Shrew. Measure for Measure* is complicated."

"No, it isn't," Beebe said.

"I don't mean complicated for people like you and me."

"It's a wonderful play," Beebe said. She loved plays where a beautiful and clever young woman is the heroine. "Isabella has such great lines like, 'O, it is excellent / To have a giant's strength; but it is tyrannous / To use it like a giant.'"

How wonderful it would be to play Isabella, pleading with the wicked Angelo (Dave Mitchell), who was trying to seduce her. But she guessed *that* play would be considered too sexy for a high school production.

"I mean," said her mother, "it's a complicated play for a person who's never seen Shakespeare before. But that's the only one that's playing next weekend."

"You mean this guy has actually never *seen* a Shakespeare play?" Beebe said disapprovingly.

Her mother nodded and laughed. "It is incredible, isn't it? But he thinks it's just as incredible that I've never gone to a football game."

"I've never gone to a football game either," Beebe said stubbornly, "and I don't think I ever will."

Her mother unplugged the iron, hung the dress up again on the door, and said, "That's what's so strange. I never thought I'd ever go to one either, but you know it was kind of fun."

Beebe snorted.

"No, really, it was exciting and colorful, and it had a kind of medieval quality to it. I bet the tournaments were like that with the knights bashing each other around and the colorful banners hanging everywhere."

"I can't believe this, Mom."

"I had a good time, Beebe," her mother said. "And Jim—well, he was really a lot of fun. He's got such a boyish sense of humor, and he entered into the whole thing, cheering and jumping up and down and giving me what he called 'high fives' every time his team did something good. Do you know what a high five is, Beebe? It's—"

"Of course I know what a high five is," Beebe said loftily. "All the jocks around school are always giving each other high fives."

Her mother said carefully, "Sometimes I think we're just a little bit too serious, Beebe. Sometimes I think maybe we don't know how to have a good time."

"I know how to have a good time," Beebe said, hurt. "You never thought we were too serious before."

"I think I'll wear the blue dress," her mother said, quickly changing the subject.

There were other questions Beebe wanted to ask her mother. She wanted to know what they had talked about and if he had . . . if he had kissed her, and, if he had, had she liked it? She followed her mother as she carried the dresses back to the closet in her bedroom. She wasn't used to being left out of her mother's life.

"What's his name?" she finally said. That wasn't the question she wanted to ask.

"Oh, Jim—Jim Driscoll."

"That sounds kind of familiar."

"He owns a hardware store out on Anza. It's called Capital Hardware. I don't think I've ever gone into it, but it's not too far away. Actually, I need some shower-curtain rings, so maybe I'll just drop in one day after work. He stays open late on Wednesdays and . . ."

Her mother was chattering away, not telling her what she wanted to know. But she seemed pleased that Beebe had shown a little interest. "He's had that store for years and he loves the work. He's very mechanical. Did I tell you he has a son about your age who also goes to Washington?"

"Yes, you told me."

"Actually, his son has just come to stay with him. He

lived with his mother until now. Jim's a little concerned about his son because he's also kind of serious."

"What do you mean 'also'?"

"Now Beebe, don't make a fuss over nothing. You know you're serious. I'm serious too. There's nothing wrong with being serious. Intelligent people often are. I wasn't criticizing you."

Her mother leaned over the chest in her bedroom and examined her face in the mirror. She smiled at her face, and Beebe thought to herself, Yes, he's kissed her, and she liked it.

New moon tonight! Odd name, Mark thought, as he stood shivering on the top of Mount Tam one cold, windy, early morning in late November with six other members of the City Astronomers, their telescopes pointed up at the sky.

New moon, when the face of the moon is hidden from the earth, and its light no longer obscures the night sky. It should be called *dark moon* or *no moon* because *new moon* sounds as if it describes a brand-new, freshly scrubbed moon beaming brightly down from the sky.

"There's one," Dr. Ridler cried, pointing up to a brilliant streak of light.

"It's early," said Jack Rogers, shining a flashlight on his watch. "It's not even one-thirty."

"Was it reddish?" another member asked. "Do you think it was an Andromedids meteor?"

"Yes! Yes!" Dr. Ridler's voice was unequivocal. "The meteor was red, and so was its train."

"Darn it!" said Helen Jackson. "I was busy fiddling with my mount—it's so stiff. I need to oil it. I hate missing an Andromedids meteor. Of course, I did see the great Leonids meteor shower back in 1966. The sky was so beautiful, I still cry when I think of it. The estimate was one hundred and fifty thousand per hour visible to the naked eye, but it was much more than that. I felt, when I saw it—this is the most beautiful sight I have ever seen in my whole life, and ever will see."

"It's going to return again in 1999," Mark said. "Maybe it will be just as wonderful then."

"Maybe," Helen Jackson said doubtfully. She was an old woman in her seventies, and Mark wondered if she thought she might not be around to see it.

He moved his telescope to get a better look at Saturn. How lovely it was with its three circling rings—the outer ring, plaited like a woman's braid; the middle ring, brightest and most interesting to him; and the inner ring, dim and transparent.

There. He found it. He marveled at its beauty as he always did. The night was so dark and clear that Saturn seemed particularly sharp and spectacular.

Helen Jackson was speaking earnestly to somebody about the superiority of the equatorial telescope mounting with a clock drive over an altazimuth mounting. He stayed out of the discussion since he had made his own mounting, a simple Dobsonian, and he knew it was too modest to mention.

A gust of wind blew his hair, and he could feel his ears stiffening with cold. He should have worn a hat. His fingers too, tightening on the scope, felt almost frozen. But he was happy, happier than he had been in a long time. The night sky in San Francisco had been foggy, or hazy when not foggy, and this was the first night since he had moved to his father's apartment that the sky had been so clear and bright.

Was that a Terby White Spot on the middle ring of Saturn? Yes, he thought it was. Quickly he checked his watch—1:53. Then he looked again. Yes, it was still there.

"There's a Terby White Spot on the B ring of Saturn," he called out, and some of the members quickly turned their scopes to check.

"Yes, there it is," Helen Jackson cried. "Very clear. What time did you catch it?"

"One fifty-three," he answered proudly as the group joined him in exclamations of admiration.

There was so much to look at tonight—the bright yellow star, Capella; the cluster of the Pleiades; the big constellation of Taurus with its red eye; and then, far, far, far off in the heavens, the faint spot of the Andromeda galaxy, like a little smudge, over two million light-years away—another galaxy like our own, another place with planets, suns, meteors, and maybe people standing on a mountain with telescopes pointed at our galaxy, and thinking about that tiny spot that they could barely find in the lenses of their telescopes.

Mark straightened up and took a deep breath of the cold air. He felt dizzy, felt himself suddenly a part of the movement in space, in time, in something beyond his own comprehension. Here was our own planet, circling the sun, and our own moon, circling our planet. Here were other planets circling the sun with their own moons circling them. And then our sun, and other stars moving too, circling the center of our own galaxy, as out there in the Andromeda galaxy and in all the other unknown galaxies, everything and everybody circling, endlessly circling.

How small he was, Mark thought, and unimportant in the whirling enormity of space. It was frightening to be so small and helpless, and heading . . . he didn't know where . . . in circles that never met.

Dr. Ridler was laughing. "Pegasus really does look like a horse," she was saying, "but not one you'd want to bet on in the Kentucky Derby."

Somebody laughed, and Mark turned back to his telescope, moving it in the direction of Pegasus. Yes, it was frightening to be such a small and unimportant speck in this whirling, endlessly circling universe—but wasn't he lucky that he was?

The phone was ringing. It penetrated his dream, and he turned over on the other side, pulled his blanket over his head, and went on dreaming.

Later, when he woke up and made his way into the kitchen, he found his father reading the Sunday paper over a cup of coffee. The clock above the refrigerator said ten-thirty. His father looked up and grinned at him.

"Late night?" he asked.

"Very late!" Mark said, grinning back. "I didn't get home until after four."

"Man," said his father, "I hope it was worthwhile."

"It sure was." Mark dropped a couple of pieces of bread into the toaster, and took a container of milk out of the refrigerator.

His father continued to grin. "I hope somebody's talking to you about taking care of yourself."

Mark felt his ears grow warm. He poured himself a glass of milk, not facing his father, facing the kitchen sink, and said quickly, "It wasn't that kind of evening, Dad. I told you I was going with the City Astronomers up to Mount Tam to look at the stars."

"Well, that's what you *said.*" His father's voice was heavy with laughter and disbelief.

"But I meant it." Mark finished pouring his milk and turned towards his father. "You saw me take my telescope, and I told you I was being picked up by somebody in the club."

"Sure, sure!" His father waved a hand. "But I didn't know who was picking you up, and who you were going to be watching with. Listen, Mark, I can remember myself doing a little stargazing with a girl when I was your age. Not that I—not that either of us knew anything about the stars—but we sure learned a lot about other things. So come on, Mark, don't tell me there aren't any cute girls in this group of yours."

Mark set the glass of milk on the table, opposite his father. "Well, there is one nice-looking woman—Dr. Ridler. She's a dentist, and she's about your age. And then, there's Ms. Jackson, not so good-looking but pretty smart. She's in her seventies. She's the one who picked me up. She's built a couple of telescopes, and knows a lot about mountings. The rest of the group are men. I guess I'm the youngest."

"Your mother called," his father said. "She said you should call her as soon as you get up. Then I want to ask you something."

Mark went off to the hall and called his mother. She picked it up after half a ring.

"Hello," she said eagerly. "Hello."

Mark felt guilty. He hadn't called her for nearly a week, and he pictured her sitting there, waiting for the phone to ring, waiting for him, and waiting.

"Hi, Mom," he said. "I was going to call you today. I was out stargazing last night, and I got in late, but I was going to call you as soon as I got up."

"I just didn't want to miss you, honey," said his mother in her important, hurried voice. "We're having Jeddy's party today instead of next weekend so I just hope you can make it. I tried to call last night—we changed the date yesterday because his scout group is going on an overnight next weekend, and I didn't know until yesterday so . . ."

"Jeddy's party?" Mark said.

"For his birthday," his mother explained. "It's really next Sunday, of course, but he'll be with his scouts. Oh, Mark, I sure hope you can make it.

He'll die if you're not there. All of his friends are coming."

"Well, sure," Mark said. "Sure, I can make it." He had forgotten Jeddy's birthday. But as long as his mother or Jeddy didn't know . . . "The only thing is, I haven't bought him a present yet. I was going to get some parts for a telescope but I didn't know the party would be today."

His mother's voice dropped. "Well, I picked up a couple of things yesterday. You can give him either a red sweat suit or a new mitt."

"I was going to build a telescope with him," Mark said. "I promised I'd build a telescope with him."

"Well, maybe next year," said his mother. "He's only interested in baseball these days anyway. Why don't you give him the mitt? I'll wrap it up for you, and you get over here as soon as you can. It's going to be a lunch party. It will start at one."

"Okay, Mom, great. Thanks, Mom. I'll get moving right away. See you soon."

His father smiled and nodded at him when he returned to the kitchen. "Everything okay?" he asked. "She only said you should call her back. She never wastes any words on me."

"Sure, Dad, everything's fine. She wants me to come out today because—"

"Oh, no," said his father. "I was hoping you'd spend the day with me."

"I'm sorry, Dad, but it's Jeddy's birthday."

"Birthday?" his father repeated. "Jeddy's birthday?"

"Of course, it's really next Sunday," Mark said quickly, knowing that his father had also forgotten, and not wanting to show that he'd noticed. "But he's going on an overnight with the scouts next weekend so Mom decided to have the party today."

"Oh right," said his father. "It's next week. That's why I was surprised."

"She wants me to come over right away. The party's starting at one. I was wondering if you're going to need the van today. It will take me three times as long if I go by BART."

"I was hoping you'd spend the day with me," said his father. "With me and Barbara and her daughter. We're going to drive out to Tiburon, have lunch, and maybe take the ferry over to Angel Island if there's time. She and her daughter like to hike around Angel Island."

"It sounds great, Dad, and I'd really love to go, but it is Jeddy's birthday party. I've never missed one of his birthday parties, and Mom says . . ."

"Sure, sure," said his father. "That's more important. Maybe I'll give you some money for Jeddy, and you can tell him he can buy anything he likes with it."

Mark didn't say anything. His father always sent money and told them to buy what they liked, but Mom never let them spend it all. Usually she gave them just a little bit of it and spent the rest on clothes or things they needed.

"Do you think he'd like that?" his father asked.

"I don't know, Dad," Mark told him. "Maybe he'd like you to buy him something."

"Like what?" his father said helplessly. "What's he interested in? Is he like you? Does he like astronomy and telescopes?"

"No," Mark said. "Right now, all he's interested in is baseball."

"Great, great," said his father. "I'll take him to some games next year. That's what I'll do. I'll write him a letter. You can take it with you, and I'll tell him we've got a date—more than one date—we'll work it out. And tell him I'll definitely take him to opening night—to a tailgate party—that's what I'll do. Tell him—never mind—I'll tell him myself."

"He'll like that," Mark said as his father stood up. "He'll really like that. But Dad I guess that means you'll need the van today."

"No, not necessarily," his father said. "Barbara's got a car—one of those little subcompacts. Maybe we can take her car, and then you can have the van."

"Well, I don't want to create any problems."

"She's not like that, Mark," his father said earnestly. "She's a real up-front kind of woman. I never felt so comfortable with anybody before. I mean she's real smart but she doesn't throw it around, and she's kind of like a kid. I guess she's had a rough time of it. Her husband died—he had leukemia—and she's been on her own ever since with a daughter to take care of. She's no whiner, but I can see she hasn't had an easy time of it, and everything we do, every place we go, it's new to her."

"You sound like you like her a lot," Mark said uneasily.

His father nodded. "I do, Mark," he said. "I like her a lot. I don't know what she thinks about me. I mean, I know she likes me. I know she has a good time with me. She looks at me sometimes when I'm talking to her, and there are lights in her eyes. I swear, Mark, there are lights in her eyes, and her cheeks get pink. She's so . . . so . . . sweet. I never met anybody like her."

He's got it bad, Mark thought, and there was a hurt place inside of him. Was it for his mother? Or was it for himself because no girl had ever looked at him with lights in her eyes?

His father had stopped talking and was standing there, lost in some kind of reverie that did not include Mark.

"So about the van?" Mark resumed.

"Oh, right, right. Just wait a minute, Mark. I'll give her a ring."

Mark busied himself over his breakfast. He smeared some peanut butter on his toast and ate standing up. He could hear his father's voice from the hall.

". . . too bad but he really has to go to Jeddy's birthday party. If he can take the van he could get there a lot faster. . . . Oh, great . . . you'll pick me up then in about twenty minutes, and you'll bring your daughter too? Great! I really want to meet her. Okay . . . okay . . . I'll tell him."

Mark started washing his dishes as his father came

back into the room. "You can have the van, Mark. She's going to pick me up. Her kid's coming too. She said to tell you she's sorry she won't get to meet you, and she hopes she will soon."

"I hope to meet her too," Mark said politely.

"Maybe I can invite her over to dinner next weekend. Maybe we can invite them both over. Maybe Saturday, after work. No. That would be too pressured. How about if we invite them both over next Sunday? I can cook my famous steak a la Driscoll, and you—what can you make?"

"How about a salad? And I can also make chocolate chip cookies."

"Great, great! So what do you say, Mark? How about Sunday?"

"Sure, Dad. I'm free Sunday."

"If her daughter's anything like her, I bet you'll really like her."

"Right, Dad." Mark was thinking maybe he'd call Cindy as soon as he got to San Leandro. Maybe she'd be home tonight. He could get together with her after the party, and they could talk about what's been happening. Maybe catch up on each other's life. She was always interested in what he had to say. She was always a real good listener, but he couldn't remember—maybe he just hadn't noticed—but he couldn't remember if he'd ever seen lights in her eyes.

7

"Thank you," Beebe said, and tried not to laugh. Jim was helping her off the ferry as if she were some kind of cripple. He was using two hands to help ease her over the small crack between the boat and the dock. Her mother had already been safely transported onto land, and stood smiling indulgently behind him.

"All set?" Jim asked, bending over her, examining her face to make sure she hadn't suffered any damage.

Her mother laughed out loud. "Stop babying her, Jim. She's as tough as you are."

He straightened up. Tall man, Beebe thought approvingly, and good-looking, too, for his age.

"And stronger than she looks," her mother continued. "You should see her tote four bags of groceries at one time. Show him your muscles, Beebe."

"Oh, Mom!" Beebe protested, but she pushed the sleeve of her sweater all the way up her arm and clenched her fist. Jim put a finger out to touch the muscle.

"Oh, my God!" he cried, shrinking back in mock terror and smiling a crooked smile that made Beebe laugh. He really was a nice man.

"I'm not used to girls," he said, taking each of them by an arm and steering them towards the island. "Especially little, strong ones."

"And we're not used to boys," Beebe's mother said. "Especially big, noisy, male chauvy ones."

"Who's a male chauve?" Jim asked, giving her arm a shake. She said something back, and for a few moments Beebe felt like the extra spoke on the wheel. But only for a few moments. Jim quickly turned his attention to her. "My daughter is twelve," he said. "I don't see her as much as I'd like." He hesitated for a moment, and then said slowly, "I guess I don't know her as well as I do Mark. He's my big boy, and I guess I even know Jeddy, the little one—he's nine— better than Marcy. I guess I just understand boys better."

"That's perfectly natural," Beebe said kindly. "I suppose a woman will always understand a girl better than a boy, and vice versa."

Jim's face was thoughtful. "The funny thing was—I felt a lot closer to my mother than to my father. There were only two of us, my sister and me, but I never felt close to him."

"Did your sister feel closer to your father?" Beebe asked.

"No, she didn't. She hated all of us," Jim said, grinning.

"She was probably jealous," said Beebe's mother. "I'll bet your mother babied you. I know my mother babied both my brothers, but she expected me to act like a grown-up by the time I was six years old. I was always jealous of my brothers."

"Well, didn't you baby Beebe?" Jim asked.

"Baby Beebe? No, I don't think I did," said her mother. "Did I, Beebe? Did I ever baby you?"

Beebe found it a difficult question to answer. Her mother had certainly always been there, was always interested and involved in her life, always ready to listen and advise—but, in a funny way, her mother had always expected her to act like a grown-up too. "No," she agreed. "No, you never did baby me."

"Okay, so now that we're finished with that topic of conversation," Jim said, "tell me why your name is Beebe. I know it's really Beatrice."

Beebe made a face.

"Uh uh," Jim said. "Am I asking a dangerous question?"

"No," said her mother. "Beebe is named after one of Shakespeare's heroines—Beatrice in *Much Ado About Nothing.* She's the smartest and the most delightful of all of Shakespeare's heroines except maybe for Portia in *The Merchant of Venice.*"

"Juliet is smart," countered Beebe.

Her mother dismissed Juliet with a wave of her hand. "Too young," she said. "Too soupy and adolescent. She's only fourteen when she dies so she's not really fully developed."

"Well, how about Lady Macbeth? She's smart."

"And wicked too," said her mother. "I wasn't about to name a child of mine after Lady Macbeth."

"You could have named me Viola after Viola in *Twelfth Night*. She's smart. And what about Isabella in *Measure for Measure?*"

Beebe's mother made a face. "Too pure for my taste, and not exactly delightful."

"I like her," Beebe insisted stubbornly. "And what did you think of her?" She turned to Jim, who was looking off in the distance.

"Uh who?" Jim asked.

"Isabella, the girl in *Measure for Measure,* that play Mom took you to."

Jim stood silently for a moment. Then he shook his head. "Which one was Isabella?"

"Oh, never mind," her mother said quickly. "And anyway, to answer your question, when Beebe was a baby, she couldn't say Beatrice. She called herself Beebe, and we just got into the habit of calling her that."

When they got home that night, Beebe's mother said, "You don't have to know anything about Shakespeare to be a good, decent human being."

"I didn't say you did," Beebe protested. "I really

like Jim. He's fun, and he's a nice guy, and I can see he really likes you."

"Yes, he does," said her mother slowly. "And I like him too, but . . ."

"He really was very sweet to me," Beebe said. "To tell you the truth, I wasn't exactly looking forward to the day, especially when I heard his son wasn't coming. But he really made sure I didn't feel left out."

"Everybody can't be crazy about Shakespeare," her mother continued. "Did you see how bored he got when we started talking about the plays?"

"Sure I did. And I really put my foot in my mouth when I asked him what he thought about Isabella. I'm sorry, Mom, but you were smart to change the subject."

"He forgot all about the play." Her mother was frowning. "I probably remembered more about his dumb football game than he remembered about *Measure for Measure.*"

"Well, you *said* it was a complicated play, remember? Maybe next time you can take him to *Twelfth Night* or *A Midsummer Night's Dream.*"

"I don't think he'd enjoy any of them. But," her mother shrugged, "everybody can't enjoy Shakespeare."

"That's right, Mom. A lot of people don't. You said Dad didn't when you first met him."

"Yes, but afterwards he really got to love him."

"The new advisor, Ms. Drumm," Beebe said, "she doesn't love Shakespeare. I don't think she even understands him. We have to keep stopping and explaining the speeches to her, and on Friday she said she was going to talk to Mrs. Kronberger and make a few big changes. I'm getting nervous about her."

"Well, don't forget," her mother said. "We've been invited over to Jim's house next Sunday night for dinner, and we'll meet his son. Jim says he's very interested in astronomy."

"Astronomy?" Beebe tried to remember something she'd heard about somebody else who was interested in astronomy. But her mind wandered off to act 3, scene 1, which the cast was to rehearse tomorrow. She thought of Romeo's speech to Tybalt—

"I do protest I never injur'd thee,
But love thee better than thou canst devise"

—and saw Dave Mitchell standing there, pleading with Tybalt and the murderous Capulets for peace. She would appear in the act too, although she'd have no speaking part, and would only be expected to stagger and go into a semi-collapse when the prince banishes Romeo.

"It could be the coach," Ms. Drumm said the next day. "The coach instead of a prince. The coach could throw Romeo off the team for fighting with Tybalt. Romeo doesn't have to kill Tybalt, just maybe knock him down."

Some of the kids on the stage looked at each other doubtfully. Beebe tried not to burst out laughing.

"And instead of old-fashioned costumes, the kids would wear school jackets. The Capulets go to Capulet High School, and the Montagues go to Montague High School. I like the idea of bright green jackets for the Capulets with the names in black, and white jackets for the Montagues with the names in purple or maybe red."

"What about Juliet?" Jennifer asked. "Is she going to be a quarterback?"

Now everybody, including Beebe, began to laugh. Jennifer made believe she was throwing a football, and Dave yelled out, "It's a . . . it's a . . . touchdown." Beebe was laughing so hard now she had to gasp for breath.

Ms. Drumm was laughing too. "It is funny, isn't it?" she said finally.

"You've got to be kidding, Ms. Drumm," Wanda yelled out.

Ms. Drumm continued laughing, but finally she stopped, stood up, and said, "No, no, I'm not kidding."

Now most of the kids stopped laughing and waited.

Ms. Drumm nodded happily at them. "It is a funny idea—I want it to be a funny idea. I've been talking to a lot of people, and nobody has ever done a funny version of *Romeo and Juliet.*"

"What about *West Side Story?*" somebody asked.

Ms. Drumm waved her hand. "I took out a video of it this weekend. It's not funny. And it's a musical. Maybe if we had time, we could do a musical too. But

West Side Story is just as heavy as *Romeo and Juliet.* Everybody dies at the end. No, no, I want to turn the whole thing into a comedy."

"But the play isn't a comedy," Beebe cried. She wasn't laughing now.

"Well—we'll change parts. It's too long, anyway. I've been thinking about it, and here's my idea. You have these two teams from two different high schools—the Capulets and the Montagues. And Juliet is a cheerleader for the Capulets. We'll have to add some other good girl parts and have some more cheerleaders for both sides. I've already spoken to Ms. Tan—she trains the cheerleaders, and she's promised to work with us. . . ."

"But . . . but . . ." Beebe cried. "That won't be Shakespeare."

"Well, not exactly. But we can keep a number of the speeches. Like in the balcony scene. It could take place in the Capulets' stadium at night, after a big game. Romeo is the best quarterback on the Montagues, and he's noticed this cute cheerleader for the Capulets. . . ."

"Ms. Drumm, Ms. Drumm," Beebe yelled as loud as she could. "I don't think Mrs. Kronberger would approve."

Ms. Drumm stopped speaking.

"She just would not approve," Beebe continued. She was still yelling even though it had grown very quiet. "Mrs. Kronberger has been putting on Shakespeare plays here for years and years. The school is famous for the plays. She would never approve if we made *Romeo and Juliet* into a comedy."

Now some of the kids on the stage were murmuring their approval of Beebe's speech. Dave Mitchell stepped over to where she stood, and said, "People from all over the city come to see our plays. We're supposed to be a model for other schools. Mrs. Kronberger always says kids can enjoy Shakespeare, that you don't have to water his plays down. And she's proved it. Last year, when we did *Twelfth Night,* we had to do three more performances, and the mayor's wife came to one of them."

Now the murmur began to swell. Beebe looked up into Dave's face with total worship, and he smiled down into hers and patted her on the shoulder.

Ms. Drumm said solemnly, "Yes, this school certainly owes a great deal to Mrs. Kronberger. She has done a marvelous job of putting this school on the map. She is certainly a marvelous person and a marvelous teacher, and we'll never forget all the work and time she's devoted to those plays. There's nobody like her—and I think it would be very nice if we sent her a card."

"We've already sent her a card," Jennifer said.

"Well, maybe another card to let her know we're thinking of her."

"When . . . when is she coming back?" Beebe asked.

"Well . . . well . . . it's very sad . . . and I didn't want to say anything until she was absolutely sure, but it's definite now that she won't be coming back. So that's why I thought we should send her another card."

Beebe felt so frightened, her legs began trembling, and she wondered if she was going to fall. She swayed, and Dave Mitchell put an arm around her shoulder. It should have made her unbearably happy, but it did not. The fear inside her grew and grew until there wasn't any room for anything else.

"But . . ." somebody began behind her. The sentence remained unfinished. Beebe felt her life would remain unfinished, too, if Mrs. Kronberger did not return. She had planned on taking Mrs. Kronberger's honors Shakespeare class next year, and she had planned on trying out for next year's play, whatever it was. Mrs. Kronberger did not know Beebe either as a student or as an actress. She knew her vaguely as somebody who had been picked to play minor parts in both plays Beebe had tried out for, but not as Beebe Clarke, who loved Shakespeare and wanted to be a great Shakespearean actress. She needed Mrs. Kronberger to put the stamp of approval on her. She needed Mrs. Kronberger to say, "Yes, Beebe Clarke, you will be a great Shakespearean actress one day, and in the meantime, I will take an interest in you because you love Shakespeare as I do. . . ."

Ms. Drumm was speaking, coaxing. ". . . a little time. Nobody can take Mrs. Kronberger's place so why not do something different? Why not have a little fun? We'll come up with a real cute play, and I bet you Mrs. Kronberger will come to a performance and get a big kick out of it. We'll just take a little time to think this through. I've been talking to Ms. Henderson in the P.E. department, and a couple of other teachers. . . ."

Dave bent over Beebe and whispered in her ear. "Let's get together afterwards and discuss this. I'll tell Jenny and Todd. Meet in front of the main entrance at four."

Seven of them gathered on the steps in front of the entrance. Wanda was the only one smiling. "A bunch of conspirators, that's what we look like," she said. "It's like out of *Julius Caesar,* not *Romeo and Juliet.*"

"She must be crazy," Jennifer said. "Nobody's going to want to act in such a nutty play. I think we should just go talk to the principal and tell him we want another faculty advisor."

"Absolutely," Dave agreed. "If a bunch of us go, he'll know we mean business."

"Maybe we should write up a petition first," Rebecca Chin suggested. "If we could have everybody in the cast sign it, that would make it unanimous."

"I think we should talk to Ms. Drumm first," Todd Merster said. "It doesn't seem fair to go behind her back before we really tell her what we think."

"I wonder if everybody in the cast would sign a petition anyway," Rebecca said. "There's a couple of them who have no principles at all. As long as they get a part in a play, they don't care what play it is."

"You're right," Robin Vargas said. "Dorrie Ferguson was telling me yesterday that she hates *Romeo and Juliet,* and just wished we could do something more modern."

• 77 •

"I know," Rebecca said. "She wanted the part of the nurse, but she's just not very funny."

"Maybe Todd is right," Jennifer said. "We should talk to Ms. Drumm first, but then, if she says no, then we should go see the principal."

"But suppose she just throws you out of the play before you go to see the principal? Suppose she just says if you don't like it you can lump it?" Wanda said.

"She wouldn't throw Jenny out of the play," Todd said, but he sounded nervous. "She wouldn't want to throw Jenny out of the play because then Dave would quit, and I guess the rest of us would quit too. She doesn't want to get rid of all of us, does she?"

Everybody was speaking at the same time now, and Beebe had to repeat herself before anybody heard her.

"What did you say, Beebe?" Dave asked finally.

"I said I'm going to see Mrs. Kronberger. I'm going to tell Mrs. Kronberger what's happening. She'll do something."

Mark's mother dropped into a chair, lighted another cigarette, breathed in deeply, slowly exhaled, and said, "Thank God that's over."

Mark watched the smoke mushroom out. "It wasn't that bad," he said.

His mother shook her head, took another deep breath, and said, "It's a good thing you were here. Twelve nine-year-old boys is not my idea of a good time."

There was a loud thump from upstairs.

"Just you stop that, Jeddy," his mother shouted up at the ceiling.

Jeddy came into the room from the kitchen. "I didn't do that," he complained. "You're always yell-

ing at me to stop something, and most of the time it's
Marcy or . . . or . . ." He looked at Mark. "It used to
be Mark."

Mark grabbed him and began tickling him. "Poor,
little, innocent lamb," he said. "He never makes any
noise, and everybody blames him."

Jeddy, yelling and laughing at the same time, tried
to butt Mark in the stomach. In a second, both of them
were rolling around together on the floor, and Mark's
mother cried, "Stop it! Both of you, stop it! Or go
outside."

There was another loud thump from upstairs, and
this time Mark's mother shouted up at the ceiling,
"Marcy, stop it!"

"Shauna and I are practicing our gymnastics,"
Marcy yelled down the stairs.

"Well, go practice in Shauna's house, and the two
of you boys, stop making that racket—watch out,
you're knocking over the lamp! Watch out!"

It took some time, but Marcy finally did go off to
Shauna's house, Jeddy went to his room with all his
new presents, and Mark and his mother remained qui-
etly together in the living room.

Mark looked anxiously at the ashtray full of cigarette
butts and at the new pack of cigarettes his mother was
opening. "Mom," he said, "aren't you smoking more
than you used to?"

She slowly pulled a cigarette out of the pack, lighted
it, took a puff, and smiled at him. "Just look out for
yourself, Mark," she said. "I can look after myself."

"I know, Mom, but I also know you're smoking a lot more than you used to."

"You don't know anything," she said, not smiling now. "It's not like you live here anymore, or take an interest in me or the kids. This is the first time you've been home in weeks."

"Mom . . ." he said helplessly.

"I'm sorry," she said. "I shouldn't have said that. You're entitled to your own life."

"Mom . . ."

"No, no." She waved a hand at him. "It's good for you to make your own way. I know you'll have to look out for yourself living with your father."

"Mom . . . that's not fair. He's really very good to me. He . . . he . . . really cares about me, and Jeddy and Marcy too."

His mother flicked some ashes into the ashtray, smiled a phony smile at him, and said, "So, Mark, tell me what's happening to you. I want to hear everything."

Jeddy came into the room, carrying one of his new games. "Mom, can I go over to Brian's house? He says I can sleep over."

"Tomorrow's school," his mother said, "and you haven't done your homework."

"I'll do it over there. Please, Mom."

"You'll have to change your clothes."

"Okay, Mom, I'll change my clothes."

"And take a shower first."

Jeddy was already out of the room.

"You never used to let me sleep over at anybody's house on a Sunday night," Mark said.

His mother shrugged. "I'm not so fussy anymore. Maybe I was too fussy with you. Maybe if I hadn't been . . ."

"Mom . . ." he began again. Today he noticed that most of his sentences began with "Mom" and didn't necessarily have any middles or ends.

"Anyway . . ." she stubbed out the cigarette, picked up the pack, hesitated, and laid it down again without taking out a new cigarette. She smiled at him, and he smiled back. Then she leaned towards him, and took his hand. "So tell me what's happening. How's school? How are you managing?"

"Fine. Everything's just fine."

His mother nodded, pressed his hand, and waited for details.

"I . . . I went up to Mount Tam last night with a club called the City Astronomers. We stayed out until three and we saw—"

"Until three?" his mother repeated, dropping his hand. "And your father didn't mind?"

"Mom . . ."

The phone rang. His mother rose quickly and headed towards it. Mark leaned back against his chair, wondering when he could go over to Cindy's. He'd called her, and she said she would be home all evening. He knew he'd have to eat dinner with his mother, and he just hoped she wouldn't feel offended if he left soon afterwards so he could spend some time with Cindy. He wondered if Cindy would be willing to meet him in the city some time—maybe next Sunday. No, next Sunday wouldn't be any good because his father was inviting Barbara and her daughter over. Well, maybe the following week.

"Mark," his mother called out, "come here a minute." He heard her say something, laughing into the phone, and she raised a smiling face up to him, still cheered by the conversation she was having with the person on the other side of the line. "Mark, how long are you staying tonight?"

"Oh—well—I don't know."

"Were you planning to have dinner?" His mother was asking him if he *planned* to have dinner. Not telling him she was expecting him to stay for dinner, not making him feel he had to stay because she expected him to.

"Well, if you want me to stay . . ." he said tentatively.

She covered up the phone with her hand. "Mark, it's up to you. If you have other plans . . ."

"Well, I was planning on seeing Cindy."

"Fine," she said. "So you're not staying for dinner. I'm free," she announced into the phone. "What? Oh sure. Eight? Yes, that's okay. Jeddy is sleeping over at a friend's, and Marcy . . . well, I'll tell her to be home before I leave. She doesn't mind staying alone for a few hours."

When she hung up, she had a cheerful look on her face.

"Is that a new boyfriend, Mom?" Mark asked, trying to look cheerful, too, and approving. Actually, he felt neglected and sorry for himself. His own mother asking him if he *planned* on staying for dinner!

"No, no," said his mother. "I'm taking a sabbatical from men this year. That's Eleanor—oh, you don't know her. She's a new friend I met through group therapy. She's having some people over for dinner— sort of potluck. I can bring some leftover birthday cake." She moved into the dining room, where the remains of the party still littered the table and the floor. "I guess I'd better clean up first before I go. I hate to come back to a messy house."

"I'll help you, Mom," Mark offered.

"No, no, dear," said his mother. "You're going off to see Cindy. Real nice girl, Cindy."

"But Mom . . ."

She looked at her watch. "I think I'd like to wash my hair before I go tonight, and maybe shorten a new skirt I bought. So you just run along. You'll be late for dinner at Cindy's if you hang around here much longer. I know they like to eat early."

He grabbed a hamburger and some fries at McDonald's, and mused over a large Coke until seven. It was incredible that his own mother no longer seemed like his own mother. Could she have changed so much in the short time he'd been away from home—from his old home? Not only was she smoking more, but she seemed much more lax with the kids. He'd hated how strict she'd always been with him, and here she was letting Jeddy stay over at a friend's house on a Sunday night, and he hadn't even done his homework. Mark's mouth tightened in disapproval. He sipped his Coke and continued to consider other changes in his mother's behavior. She was going to let Marcy, twelve-year-old Marcy, stay alone in the house! Oh, come on, Mark, lighten up! It's only for a couple of hours, another side of him reasoned. But he brushed it aside and continued to work up a case against his mother. Worst of all was the way she had behaved with him, throwing recriminations at him for leaving. Well, he could deal with that. He even expected that, but—the real stunner—asking him if he *planned* to stay for dinner, and actually easing him out of the house so that she could wash her hair. His own mother!

He looked at the clock and considered whether he wanted another order of french fries or whether he wanted to call Cindy and see if he could come over earlier. He called Cindy.

"Hello," Cindy said.

"Hello," he answered.

"Hello?" she returned. "Who is this?"

"It's Mark!" he told her. She always used to know his voice.

"Oh, hi, Mark," she said enthusiastically. "I hope you're still planning on coming over tonight."

"Oh, sure, I am, but I'm through here a little early, so I thought . . ."

"We're just sitting down to dinner," she said. "You said you wouldn't be over before eight."

"Right. Well, that's okay. I'll come at eight, then."

"Unless you haven't eaten, and want to have dinner with us. I didn't ask you because I was sure your mother wouldn't let you get out of the house without stuffing you."

"Oh, I've eaten all right." Mark laughed. He didn't want her to think his own mother would let him go out of her house hungry. "I'll see you at eight."

He bought another order of french fries and another Coke, brooded some more over his mother, and arrived at Cindy's house at five minutes after eight.

"Mark!" She flung her arms around him and gave him a big hug. He could smell a combination of onions, apples, and cinnamon in her hair, and began to feel happy again.

"Mark!" Her mother was there, hugging him, and her father came and shook hands, and asked him how he was doing. Then they all trouped into the kitchen, asking questions and listening to his answers. He liked Cindy's parents, and knew they liked him.

"We really miss you, Mark," said her mother.

"And speaking of missing," said her father. "We're going to miss 'Masterpiece Theatre' unless we turn on the TV. They're doing *A Tale of Two Cities,*" he told Mark. "Have you been watching?"

"No, I haven't."

"It's great," Cindy said. "The last episode they actually showed how the guillotine worked, and you could see the blood on it." She shuddered.

"Well, maybe you want to watch it," Mark said. "I don't mind."

He could see her hesitate, but then she smiled and shook her head. "No, it's okay, Mark. I'd rather talk to you. Dad can tape it for me."

He followed Cindy upstairs to her room, approving of her no-nonsense, baggy blue sweater, baggy jeans, and scuffed running shoes. She was a tall girl—pretty, too, in a careless, sporty way. The important thing was that Cindy was a no-nonsense girl, a girl he could talk to. He hadn't realized how much he'd missed her.

She put on the light in her room, closed the door, and looked up at him. "Guess what I've been doing, Mark?"

Her eyes were bright and shining. Were there lights in them? Maybe. Yes, he thought there were.

"What?" he asked, moving a little closer to her.

"Just look." She waved a hand around the room, and he looked. All over her bed, her desk, and the tops of her bookcases were—

"College catalogs," she told him. "I got a whole bunch in the mail, some from places I've never even heard of. And some I sent for."

"No kidding!" Mark picked one up. "Stanford, Wow! Are your marks that good?"

"I guess so," she said, "and I did pretty well on the PSATs."

"What did you get?"

"Seven twenty in English and 790 in math."

"Seven ninety?" Mark pushed aside some of the

catalogs on her bed, and sat down. "If you do that well on the SATs you'll get in anywhere. I got a 710 in math and only a 650 in English."

She sat down next to him, and for the next couple of hours they talked and talked and talked. It was like old times. He could always talk to Cindy, and she could always talk to him.

"I guess I'll go to U.C. Berkeley," Mark said, "if I can get in."

"Why don't you go somewhere else, Mark? Your scores are okay, and your marks are all high. You might get into M.I.T."

"No, I want to go to Berkeley. It's a good school, and it won't cost as much."

"But maybe you'll get a scholarship."

They talked and talked, and suddenly it was nearly eleven.

"I should go," Mark said, looking at the clock.

Cindy stood up. "I wish you still lived around here," she said. "It was always easier talking to you than anybody else. But I should finish some work I have to do for chem."

Mark jumped up. "Why didn't you tell me?"

She put an arm around him and looked up at him. Yes, there were lights in her eyes, but maybe not for him. Maybe not for anybody. Maybe she just had lights in her eyes. He could still smell the onions, apples, and cinnamon in her hair. "Because," she said, "I was enjoying myself. I always enjoy myself with you."

She smiled at him, and he smiled back at her. Yes, he always enjoyed himself with her too, but they were friends. That's what they were. He had missed her because you miss a friend, and he knew he was very lucky to have a friend like Cindy.

"We should get together," he said as they walked down the stairs. "Would you meet me sometimes in the city?"

"Sure," she said. "I've got my license now. I can drive in."

"Let's set something up in a couple of weeks," he said. "And we should call each other from time to time."

"I wanted to call you," she said, "but I thought maybe you were busy with your new friends."

"No," Mark said. "I don't have any new friends—at least, I don't have any friends like you."

"No kidding?"

"No kidding."

Yes, he was very lucky, he thought as he drove home. Very lucky to have a friend like Cindy. It would be great if she came into the city. Maybe she'd like to do a little stargazing up on Mount Tam with him, although her main interest was geophysics. He definitely would call her from time to time. He was lucky to have her as a friend.

But if he was so lucky, how come he was feeling so unlucky? How come he was feeling that something terrible had happened that evening? What was it? What had happened? Nothing. That's what had happened. He had hoped—he had thought—that he and Cindy would get together, but, somehow, it hadn't happened. And that was the terrible thing that had happened.

He tried to remind himself that Cindy's friendship was a rare and precious thing, but he felt bitterly disappointed. And he knew that it was not friendship he was longing for.

A smiling man opened the door. "Hello," he said.
"I'm Roger Kronberger, Helen's husband. Come in,
come in."

"Thank you, Mr. Kronberger," Beebe said, passing
through the door and into a long, dark hallway. She
hesitated, turned back to him, and asked in a low voice,
"How is Mrs. Kronberger?"

His smile wobbled. "Oh, fine. Just fine. Here, let me
take your coat. She's in the living room, and I know
she's been looking forward to seeing you. It's very nice
of you to think of her. A number of students have
called and written. She got a marvelous letter from a
student she had fifteen years ago—one of those talented kids who's now acting in the Oregon Shakespeare Festival. She was always very proud of him."

She would have been proud of me, too, Beebe thought jealously.

Mr. Kronberger laid her coat down on a bed in a small room off the hall, and led her to the living room.

"Look who's here, Helen," he announced, his smile firm again.

Mrs. Kronberger was sitting on the sofa, a book in her hands. She closed it, took off her glasses, and smiled up at Beebe. "What a nice surprise," she said. "Come and sit down"—she patted a place on the sofa next to her—"and tell me what's been happening with the play."

Mrs. Kronberger's face looked flat and unnaturally rosy. Beebe realized that she had grown used to seeing her in the dim light of the auditorium. There, her face appeared gaunt and pale with deep, shadowy places. Here in the brightly lit room, the shadows were gone from her face, and the pink color of her skin was startling.

And she has blue eyes, Beebe thought as she seated herself in the designated spot. I always thought she had dark eyes.

The blue eyes, above a smiling mouth, were looking at her as she seated herself carefully on the sofa. "What would you like?" Mrs. Kronberger asked. "Tea . . . milk . . . or . . . Roger, do we have any soft drinks?"

"Oh, that's all right," Beebe said quickly. "I really don't want . . ."

"No, we don't," Mr. Kronberger said regretfully, "but we do have apple juice or Calistoga water."

"I really don't want anything," Beebe said solemnly. "Please don't go to any trouble."

"It's no trouble at all." Mrs. Kronberger laughed, and her husband echoed it. "We've been waiting for you, and Roger even baked some cookies."

"Oh, I really didn't want you to . . ."

Mrs. Kronberger leaned over and patted Beebe's hand. "Now, Barbie," she said, "Roger and I are dying for our tea, and we insist you have some too."

Barbie?

Mrs. Kronberger smelled like somebody sick even though she was rosy and smiling like somebody well. But it was a somebody entirely different from her usual cranky, scowling self with a face full of dark shadows.

Beebe gave in and said, "Thank you."

"So what will you have?" asked Mr. Kronberger.

"Uh—whatever you're having."

"We're having tea."

"Oh, that's just fine."

"But we do have milk."

"I'd like tea. Really, I would like tea."

"If you'd rather, you could have apple juice or Calistoga water."

It took some further exhausting insistence on Beebe's part that she really would prefer tea before Mr. Kronberger went off and left her alone with Mrs. Kronberger.

"Now then, Barbie, tell me what's happening with the play."

"Beebe," she corrected.

It was bad enough that Mrs. Kronberger didn't know her name, but that she should call her Barbie was humiliating. She didn't look like a Barbie. She didn't act like a Barbie. It was such a terrible insult that even though she knew suddenly that Mrs. Kronberger was a very sick woman, and that some allowances needed to be made, she could not allow anyone—not even a very, very sick woman—to call her Barbie.

"What?" Mrs. Kronberger's smile wavered.

"My name," said Beebe very slowly and distinctly, "is Beebe. Beebe Clarke."

"Oh dear," said Mrs. Kronberger, the smile lingering. "I always thought your name was Barbie."

"But Barbie is a terrible name," Beebe said. "It's for somebody silly and conventional, like a Barbie doll. It's not like me at all. I would hate it if my name was Barbie."

Mrs. Kronberger narrowed her blue eyes and squinted at Beebe. She also stopped smiling and began to look a little like her old self.

"It is a terrible name," she agreed, "and I apologize. Of course, Beebe is—well—that is rather an unusual name."

"It's a nickname," Beebe explained proudly. "My real name is Beatrice. It's from *Much Ado About Nothing.* My mother is an actress. She was playing Beatrice when she met my father. And that's what they called me. Only I couldn't say Beatrice when I was a baby."

Now Mrs. Kronberger picked up her glasses, put them on, and inspected Beebe's face. Her glasses were tinted, and her eyes didn't look so blue.

"Now let me see," she said, "you play—Lady Capulet, is it?"

"No," Beebe said bitterly. "I only play Lady Montague, and last year I was an attendant in *Twelfth Night.* I didn't have a speaking part, but you let me understudy Viola's role. You said since I knew it, and Viola—Jennifer—never got sick, you said it would be okay. And this year, I'm also Juliet's understudy."

"Oh yes," Mrs. Kronberger said. "You're the girl with the amazing memory."

"My memory isn't amazing," Beebe said. "I know all those lines because I read the plays so much. Over and over again. I love the plays. And so does my mother. We read them together sometimes. Out loud."

"Tell me about your mother," Mrs. Kronberger said. "What's her name? What plays has she been in?"

"Her name is Barbara Clarke—and nobody ever calls her Barbie."

"Barbara Clarke? Hmm . . . I don't think . . ."

"Oh, she hasn't acted for years—since I was born. She used to act before that. People thought she was wonderful, but my father got sick, and : . . she couldn't."

"I see," said Mrs. Kronberger. She took off her glasses and looked helplessly in the direction of the doorway. "Roger should be bringing in our tea soon. He's not the handiest man in a kitchen."

"Should I help?" Beebe began to rise.

"No, no, dear, just stay where you are, and tell me what's been happening with the play."

Beebe hesitated. She knew she shouldn't be piling all of her sorrows and disappointments onto this sick, sick woman, but that was the reason for her visit, and she was convinced that Mrs. Kronberger would want to know the truth and, knowing it, would take some very strong action. She leaned closer to Mrs. Kronberger and said, "She's ruining it! She's murdering it!"

"She's what?"

"She's destroying the play," Beebe said in a furious rush of words. "She's taking everything apart. She's changing the lines. She's adding different characters, turning it into a comedy. *Romeo and Juliet* into a comedy! And nobody can stop her. The kids—they stand around, and they complain behind her back. Some of them say they're going to the principal, and some of them talk about a petition, but every day she changes something, and nobody does anything. Yesterday, she took out those stunning lines that Romeo speaks when he thinks Juliet is dead. You know what I mean:

". . .O my love! my wife!
Death, that hath suck'd the honey of thy breath,
Hath had no power yet upon thy beauty:
Thou art not conquer'd; beauty's ensign yet
Is crimson in thy lips and in thy cheeks,
And death's white flag is not advanced there."

" 'Pale,' " said Mrs. Kronberger. "It's 'death's pale flag,' not 'white' flag."

"Are you sure?" Beebe asked. "White makes more sense since it means surrender. The white flag of surrender."

"Of course I'm sure," Mrs. Kronberger snapped. "I've known that play a lot longer than you have." She put her glasses back on, and Beebe said happily, because Mrs. Kronberger was now acting like her old, cranky, fussy, caring self, "Yes, Mrs. Kronberger, I'm sure you're right. But Mrs. Kronberger, she's destroying the play. She's violating the play. She's even written a new prologue about two schools, Capulet High School and Montague High School, and taken out the most important line in the whole play."

"What line is that?" Mrs. Kronberger demanded.

" 'A pair of star-cross'd lovers take their life,' " Beebe recited angrily. "She's substituted, 'A pair of high school kids caught in the fight.' Please, Mrs. Kronberger, you have to do something."

Mrs. Kronberger was looking at her solemnly. "Why didn't you take my Shakespeare class?" she asked.

"I was going to take it next term," Beebe answered. "I'm only a junior, and I had to get some other things out of the way first. But I was planning on taking it next year, and now . . . and now . . ."

"Now," Mrs. Kronberger finished, "now, you'll have to take it with somebody else."

"There is nobody else," Beebe said, almost accusingly. "You're the only one I wanted. You're the only one who . . . who . . ." She wanted to say, "You're the only one who knows more than I do about Shakespeare," but it sounded so conceited she just left the sentence unfinished. For a moment or two there was silence. Then Mrs. Kronberger said, "I'm not the only one. Don't make that mistake, Beebe. There's never an only one in anybody's life."

"It's not fair," Beebe said. "It's not fair."

"No," said Mrs. Kronberger, "I suppose it's not. Life is often not fair. And neither is art. Think of poor Romeo and Juliet. Art wasn't fair to them."

"But art is different from life," Beebe said. "Art can make sense of tragedy. Shakespeare's language can make suffering meaningful. It demeans his art to turn the play into some kind of slapstick comedy."

Mrs. Kronberger smiled. "You sound like a college professor, Beebe," she said. "Is that what you want to be?"

"No," Beebe said. "No. I want to be an actress."

"An actress?" Mrs. Kronberger shook her head. "Why would *you* want to be an actress?"

And there it was—the unkindest cut of all. It didn't slice into her with a dagger, but it came with the clarity of a simple, undeniable fact. Two and two are four and "Why would *you* want to be an actress?" What Mrs. Kronberger meant, of course, was why would somebody like you who was only an attendant in last year's play without a speaking part, and was only Lady Montague with just a few lines in this year's play—why would somebody without talent want to be an actress?

"My mother," Beebe murmured. "My mother wants me to be an actress."

"Yes," said Mrs. Kronberger, "lots of mothers want their children to be actresses and actors."

"But my mother thinks I'm talented. . . ."

"Yes." Mrs. Kronberger sighed and shook her head. "Lots of mothers think their children are talented."

"But if I don't become an actress," Beebe cried, "what will I do?"

"Why, you'll have to figure that one out for yourself, won't you?" said Mrs. Kronberger, almost crankily. "And getting back to *Romeo and Juliet*, what is it you want me to do?"

"Make her stop," Beebe said fiercely. "Make her do the play the right way, or get us a different faculty advisor."

At this point, Mr. Kronberger carried in a tray with a teapot, sugar, spoons, cookies, and napkins, and set it down on the coffee table in front of the sofa.

"Dear," said Mrs. Kronberger, "you've forgotten the cups, and maybe Beebe would like milk in her tea."

"No, no milk," Beebe said impatiently, and then, remembering her manners, she added, "I mean no, thank you."

"I'll be right back," Mr. Kronberger said, hurrying off.

Beebe kept her eyes on Mrs. Kronberger's face, and Mrs. Kronberger raised her eyes from the tea tray and said, almost kindly, "I'm sorry, Beebe, but there's nothing I can do."

"Why not?" Beebe demanded. "You could call Ms. Drumm and tell her to stop."

Mrs. Kronberger didn't answer. She turned her attention to the tea tray, moving the teapot to one side and picking up the plate of cookies. They were chocolate chip cookies, Beebe noticed, and some of them were burned.

"Will you have a cookie?" Mrs. Kronberger asked, smiling again and holding the plate out in Beebe's direction.

"No, thank you," Beebe said coldly. She wanted Mrs. Kronberger to know how angry and disappointed she was. It wasn't even that she had crushed Beebe's own future hopes by letting her see how hopeless she considered them to be, but that she would also sit idly by and allow Shakespeare to be dismembered.

Mrs. Kronberger picked a cookie—one that didn't seem as burned as some of the others—and put the plate down again. She took a little nibble at it and whispered, "I think he forgot to put in the vanilla."

Beebe preserved a dignified silence, and Mrs. Kronberger turned to her and asked, "Why do you think 'a pair of star-cross'd lovers take their life' is the most important line in the play?"

"Because it's what the play is all about," Beebe said. "Nothing worked right for them, not even their stars. And we know that Shakespeare wasn't big on astrology since he has Cassius say in *Julius Caesar,* 'The fault, dear Brutus, is not in our stars / But in ourselves that we are underlings.' It's just that in *Romeo and Juliet,* everything goes wrong for them, including their stars."

Beebe reached over and picked up a cookie. As she

bit into it, she realized that she had picked a burnt one.

"You could teach," said Mrs. Kronberger. "You're certainly intelligent, and you might make an excellent teacher."

"Not me," Beebe said. "I don't want to teach. I want . . . I used to want to be an actress, but now . . ."

Mr. Kronberger returned to the room with another tray containing cups, and for a while all the conversation focused on matters of eating and drinking.

"Beebe is unhappy with how the play is proceeding at school," Mrs. Kronberger said, finally, to her husband.

"I'm sorry to hear that," said Mr. Kronberger. He held out the plate of cookies to Beebe and said, "Have another cookie?"

"No, thank you," she said.

"The new faculty advisor is turning the play, *Romeo and Juliet*, into a comedy about rival high school football teams," Mrs. Kronberger continued.

"Hasn't that been done already?" Mr. Kronberger asked, picking up the teapot. "More tea anybody?"

"No, thank you," Beebe said.

"You're thinking of *West Side Story*," Mrs. Kronberger said.

"Yes, I probably am," Mr. Kronberger said, looking carefully at his wife. She set down her cup and leaned back against the sofa. Her cheeks had grown even more flushed than they were when Beebe first arrived.

"And I think Beebe wants me to interfere," Mrs. Kronberger said in a very tired voice. "And I know she's disappointed that I won't."

"Yes, well I'm really sorry to hear it," Mr. Kronberger said, rising, "and I think it's probably time for you to take your pill."

Mrs. Kronberger looked at her watch. "Oh my," she said, "is it that time already?"

Beebe understood that it was time for her to go, and she stood up and murmured that she had to get home.

"Well, it was very nice of you to come," said Mr. Kronberger, moving towards the door.

"I'm sorry, Beebe," said Mrs. Kronberger, "but I just can't get involved."

Why not? Beebe wanted to cry. Why can't you get involved? Nothing would ever stop me from getting involved, no matter how sick I was. But Mr. Kronberger had already reached the door and was smiling at her, holding her coat and waiting for her to catch up with him. So she mumbled something about the nice tea and thank you for letting her come and that she hoped Mrs. Kronberger would be feeling better and . . .

"Good luck to you, Beebe," said Mrs. Kronberger. "I hope there will be some happy stars in your future."

It wasn't until she was outside, walking home at a furious clip, that the whole force of her visit with Mrs. Kronberger struck her. She hadn't realized that Mrs. Kronberger was so sick. And she hadn't realized that she, Beebe Clarke, would never be an actress. And, above all, she had not really believed it possible that

Mrs. Kronberger would sit by and allow *Romeo and Juliet* to be destroyed.

It was a chilly December evening, and the stars were already out as Beebe, trembling under her coat, hurried homewards. Mrs. Kronberger had hoped that there would be some happy stars in her life, but at that moment she felt star-cross'd. Yes, that's what she was. Star-cross'd in everything that mattered. But she would have to find a way to stop Ms. Drumm from ruining the play. She didn't know how she would do it, but she would do it.

She could barely climb the stairs to her apartment, her teeth were chattering so and her whole body hurt. When her mother saw her face as she came inside, she cried, "Beebe what's wrong? Is something the matter?"

10

"They can't come Sunday night," his father said, "because Beebe—that's Barbara's daughter—because Beebe is sick." His father was sitting, crumpled up, near the phone.

"I'll be back in a minute," Mark said, carrying the groceries into the kitchen. His father looked so upset that he thought he should just dump the bags down on the kitchen table and hurry back. But there were a few frozen things, so first he hunted around in the bags, dug out the frozen chicken pies and the frozen sausages, and piled them into the freezer before returning to his father.

"What's wrong with her daughter?" Mark asked.

"Oh—it sounds like kind of a flu. She's running

some fever and she's coughing. No big deal. But Barbara doesn't want to leave her."

Like Mom, Mark thought approvingly, or, at least, like Mom used to be. "Well," he said, "maybe they can come the following Sunday."

His father's eyes narrowed, and his face tightened as if something was hurting him. "She could come Sunday. It's two days off. Her daughter should be a lot better by then. And I was expecting her to come. I even got a bottle of wine—one of those fancy wines the guy in the wine store said was special."

"Well, it will keep until next week, won't it, Dad?"

"I guess so."

"Anyway, Dad, what should we have for dinner tonight? I bought some frozen chicken pies and some sausages. We could have the sausages with the leftover spaghetti from yesterday. And I think there's still some French bread."

"I just can't figure her out," his father said, not rising from his chair by the phone. "In the beginning, she was always ready to get together. She never put me off."

"But Dad, her kid is sick. She's not putting you off. She's worried about her kid."

"You think that's what it is?" his father asked, his eyes widening with hope. It was embarrassing to see his father so affected. Embarrassing and troubling too. So far, there hadn't been any girl in his own life who would have crumpled him up like that in front of a phone.

"Maybe you're right," said his father, turning to the phone again and beginning to dial.

"Dad . . ." Mark began. He wanted to tell his father not to . . . not to . . . what?

"Oh—right, Mark. Let's have those sausages. Hi . . . Barbara, it's Jim again. Look, why don't we just take a rain check on that dinner—put it off a week until Beebe's feeling better. Right . . . right . . . but I was thinking . . ."

Mark went into the kitchen and began unpacking the other groceries. He put the four cans of minestrone soup into the cupboard along with the six cans of tuna and the eight cans of refried beans. He had forgotten to buy napkins again, and they'd have to use paper towels or tissues. His father may have been very organized in his hardware store, but he wasn't at all organized about grocery shopping. Increasingly, Mark had taken over the shopping because he was growing tired of eating out.

His father followed him into the kitchen, and sat down by the table. Now his face had a surly, dissatisfied look. "She won't let me do anything for her. I offered to shop or pick up drugs, but she said no. If she's so worried about leaving her kid alone for a couple of hours, how come she won't let me go shopping for her?"

"Maybe she doesn't need any shopping," Mark suggested.

"Oh she does, she does." His father sulked. "But she says a neighbor is doing it for her."

"Well, then . . ."

"She just won't let me do anything," his father said angrily. "I even offered to bring them some Chinese food so she wouldn't have to cook, but she just said no. Everything I offered to do, she said no."

"Dad," Mark said kindly, as if he were talking to somebody very young, "Dad, maybe you just have to . . ."

"Have to what?" his father snapped.

"Well—have to leave her be. Maybe you just can't crowd her now. After all, her kid is sick and . . ."

"Listen, Mark, I don't need your advice. I know a lot more about women than you do."

"I know, Dad, I know but . . ."

"So just don't tell me how to act."

"Okay, Dad, okay."

The phone rang, and his father flew out of the room. "Hello, hello," he heard his father say.

"It's for you." His father returned to the kitchen and sank back into the chair by the table.

It was a girl. "Hi, Mark," she said. "It's Wanda."

"Wanda?"

"I met you at Jennifer's party a few weeks ago, and you were telling me all about the stars. . . ."

"Oh right. Sure. I remember."

"Well, maybe you also remember I told you I had a friend who also didn't believe in astrology the way you said you didn't."

"Uh . . ."

"Anyway, her name is Beebe Clarke and . . ."

"She's sick," Mark said.

There was a pause on the other end of the line. "I didn't think you knew her."

"I don't," Mark said, and wondered how you tell somebody that the reason you know a girl you don't know is sick is because your father is dating her mother. It was beyond him, and he muttered something about a friend telling him.

"Isn't that funny. I mean, I didn't see her in school today, but I didn't know she was sick. I was going to call her after I asked you."

"Asked me what?"

"If you wanted to meet her. My boyfriend . . ." Wanda stopped to laugh with pride. "I mean, he and I have just started going out together. Actually, you met him at the party too. But we hadn't started going around together then. His name is Frank Jackson. He was up on Jennifer's deck when you and I were down in the yard."

"Well . . . I . . ."

"Tall guy with curly blond hair and sort of green eyes."

"Maybe I do remember him."

"He's going to play Capulet in the play. Only it's not Capulet anymore. But he's Juliet's father, and he's very strict. It's funny because he's really such a quiet guy, and he really has to carry on when she stays out late with Romeo."

"Right," Mark said quickly. "I remember him all right."

"Anyway, what's wrong with Beebe?"

"She's sick—maybe it's the flu. I know she has a fever and she's coughing."

"How high is her fever?"

"I really don't know," Mark said. "I just heard that she was sick."

"Who told you?"

"I forget, but anyway, why don't we put it off until she feels better?"

"Okay, but do you know if she went to the doctor?"

The conversation was getting sillier and sillier. Mark said firmly, "I don't know if she's gone to the doctor, but I have to go now."

"Okay, Mark. I'll set something up after she's better. Okay?"

"Sure. Why not?"

He returned to the kitchen. His father was standing up now, looking into the refrigerator. "What do we have for dinner, Mark?" he asked.

"Sausages and spaghetti, Dad, but listen. Something really crazy just happened."

"What?" His father half turned towards him, and tried to appear interested.

"This girl just called, and she wants to set me up with guess who?"

"I can't imagine," his father said without much enthusiasm.

"Well, listen to this, Dad. She wants to set me up with Beebe Clarke."

Now his father was interested. "With Beebe, Barbara's daughter?"

"Right. And this girl is Beebe's friend. I think she

• 109 •

said her name was Wanda. She didn't know Beebe was sick. I had to tell her and I don't even know Beebe."

Now his father was grinning. "Hey, that's a kick."

"Her friend sounds like a flake though. I hope she's not like that."

"No," said his father. "No, she's not a flake. She's a nice girl and a pretty girl. And she liked me. We got along just fine. You'll like her."

"Well, I know I'll meet her one way or another."

"Oh sure," said his father. "Maybe I'll give Barbara a ring and tell her. She'll get a kick out of it too. She's got a real good sense of humor. Kind of quiet but good."

His father looked ready to tear out of the room, and Mark said, before he could stop himself, "Dad . . ." His father winced, but he turned back towards the refrigerator and said, "Okay, Mark, okay. Now what are we eating tonight?"

Later, his father plunked himself down in front of the TV set.

"Dad, will you need the van tonight?" Mark asked, after he had washed the dishes and cleaned up the kitchen.

His father shook his head.

"Well, I was thinking of driving up to Twin Peaks and looking at the stars. Somebody in the City Astronomers said it's usually clear up there, and the view is great."

"Sure," said his father, his eyes on the TV set. "Good idea."

Mark hesitated. He wanted to do something for his father, cheer him up, make him forget his disappointment over Barbara.

"Dad," he said, "why don't you come with me?"

"No," said his father. "I've been there lots of times." But then, as if he was reminded of something, he looked up quickly at Mark, smiled, and said, "Thanks, Mark. You're a good kid, but I'm kind of bushed tonight. We were stacking cans of paint all day. It'll be your turn tomorrow. You go yourself. Maybe another time."

The fog followed him up the twisty road to the top of Twin Peaks. He could see most of it below him, wrapped around the streets and houses, dimming the lights from windows and street lamps, and even muffling the persistent red and green Christmas lights that twinkled on and off all over the city. Above him, wisps of fog obscured his views of Perseus, Cassiopeia, and Andromeda.

It was disappointing. He stood by himself on the cold, windy edge of the hill. There were others beside him up there on the top of Twin Peaks, but all of them were inside cars, and most of them were not alone.

It was disappointing. Except for that one splendid night on Mount Tam, his view of the skies had, for the most part, been obscured by fog or, if the night happened to be clear, a full moon.

He leaned against the front of the van and tried to think positively. His father was generous with the van, and his father never bugged him the way his mother did—or, at least, the way she used to. He raised his eyes to the fog now swirling more heavily above his head. It was disappointing. And suddenly, he was crying.

Nervously, he turned his head to the car on his right. Inside, he saw two heads close together. Nobody would notice him crying. Nobody would care. The tears raced down his face, and he found himself gulping for air. It was disappointing—the fog, his father—yes, his father was disappointing. He had expected—what had he expected? That his father would be his buddy, his pal, would make up for all those years of separation? His shoulders began heaving as he thought about his father, plunked down in front of the TV set, sulking because his girlfriend wouldn't put him first before her sick kid.

He tried to remember when he was small if his father had ever stayed home with him when he was sick. He could remember his mother's cool hands on his forehead when he had a fever, and his mother plumping up his pillows and playing cards with him, and making soup. . . .

His mother. It was always his mother who had taken care of him, and how had he repaid her? The tears ran all over his face now, and he wiped them away quickly with the sleeve of his jacket. How cold it was! The wind on his wet face burned, but he stayed outside of the van, all alone on top of foggy Twin Peaks.

Why had he left her? Should he go back? No. No. It was too late now for him to go back. He gulped another throatful of the cold air and tried to straighten up. His mother—she wasn't the same. She had changed. He had started a whole spiral of happenings by leaving. His mother had changed, and so had Marcy and even Jed. They were forgetting about him, and he—yes, he was forgetting about them too. His head whirled with all the changes. He felt as if he were spinning around in circles.

There was music. He could hear it faintly. It came from the car on his left—another car with two heads very close together. Well, he thought, well, standing up straight and mopping his face with his dry sleeve, you're the one who started it, and you're the one who'll have to straighten it out.

The fog was so thick now there were no more glimpses down below of the tiny streets and houses. And no more misty views of the stars and constellations up above. He might as well get back into the van and head home.

Now he could hear somebody laughing. This time it came from the car on the right. Were they laughing at him? No, of course not. He didn't exist as far as they were concerned. They were laughing into each other's faces. They didn't even notice him watching them.

Would it ever happen to him, he wondered. Would he ever be sitting up here with a girl, not caring whether or not the fog was obscuring Cassiopeia or Andromeda?

The fog was circling around him, but he began to feel better. Why not me too, he thought. Why not? Now this girl, Beebe Clarke, maybe she would be somebody for him. He tried to picture her. Cindy's face bloomed inside his head—a tall, pretty girl, well-developed but sporty. No. Didn't his father tell him that Barbara and Beebe were small and dark-haired? Another image bloomed inside his head—a lovely, slim, delicate, pale girl with long, dark hair and slender fingers, who played the piano. . . .

No. Beebe was in that acting bunch. He shook his head slightly. Maybe she would be one of those phony, affected girls who wore a lot of makeup and talked in a theatrical way. A picture of Lauren, his father's old girlfriend, with her painted face and bold look, now bloomed inside his head, and he shook it off. No. No. She wouldn't look like that. His father said she was a nice girl.

His father. He shivered and quickly got back inside the van. Looking out at the fog through the windshield of a warm car made a difference. He felt better. Beebe Clarke, whatever she looked like—maybe she would be the kind of girl he could like. And vice versa. Then, inside his head, a picture bloomed of two people walking, at a distance. They were holding hands, and the smaller one, a girl, was smiling up at the taller one, a boy. He couldn't see the girl's face clearly, but he knew who the boy was, and he felt good. If they had nothing else to talk about, they could always talk about their parents. They could talk about them and laugh together at the mess grown-ups always seem to make of their lives.

They could talk and listen, and be in love. Mark wasn't sure about what and how it happened that two people fell in love. He and Cindy hadn't fallen in love. They should have, but they hadn't. They circled each other, but never came together. And he knew now that, in love, two people came together. Mysteriously, wonderfully, they came together.

And why it happened so that up there, on the top of Twin Peaks, there were couples together in cars all around him while he was still alone he couldn't say. But he wanted it to happen, and he knew he was ready.

Mark started up the van, backed out carefully, and began the descent. His father? Well, yes, his father was a disappointment, and he knew he would never be like his father when he grew up. He would stay home with a sick kid, and he would share his kid's interests, and go with him up to Twin Peaks to look at the stars even if the night was foggy.

His father? He began to smile. A warm, indulgent feeling swirled inside of him, as the fog circled around outside, and he carefully and slowly drove down the twisty road. His father was like a kid, a big, loveable kid like Jeddy, and he was just going to have to accept him the way he was. He loved his father, and he knew his father loved him. The same was true of his mother. It wasn't enough though. But for now, he had to find his way home in all this swirling fog. That was what he had to do now.

"The fog has finally cleared," said her mother cheerfully one morning. She partially opened the blinds in Beebe's room, moved over to the bed, put her hand on Beebe's head, and said, "You're much cooler today. How do you feel?"

"Okay, I guess," Beebe murmured, licking her dry lips. "But my head still hurts."

Her mother stroked her forehead. "Poor baby," she said. "What a time you've had."

It was not only her head that hurt, it was all of her. She had never really been sick like this before, and she surrendered herself completely to the aches, pains, exhaustion, and especially to the blackout in her mind. She didn't think about anything. For the most part, she slept or drank cool drinks or let her mother move her around from the couch to the bed. She knew her mother was taking off from work to stay with her, and she burrowed deeply inside her mother's love.

"Wanda's on the phone," said her mother one evening. "Do you want to speak to her? I'll bring the phone over to the couch."

Beebe was lying awake now on the couch with the TV on. It was some kind of a talk show, and the guest specialized in raising attack dogs. Beebe was only half following the interview. She was very comfortable.

"Beebe," her mother repeated, "it's Wanda."

"Wanda?" It took Beebe a moment to remember Wanda and the world out there. "I can't," she said. "I can't."

"Beebe will call you later," she heard her mother say. "She's still kind of feverish but much better. Oh? . . . Well, I couldn't say. . . . Well, isn't that nice. . . . Better not make it this weekend though. . . . Sure . . . Sure . . . I'll tell her."

Her mother looked pleased as she returned to the room.

"Wanda sends you her love, and . . ."

Now the guest was a famous football player, and he was telling how he had broken his collarbone several times and his ribs.

"Should I turn off the set, Beebe?" her mother

asked. "I don't think you're really listening anyway."

Her mother turned off the set and sat down on the edge of the couch where Beebe lay, propped up on pillows and wrapped in a blanket.

"Wanda wants you to meet some nice boy she thinks you'd like," said her mother, smiling. "She wanted to set something up for this weekend, but I said she'd better wait another week or so."

Beebe sighed and tried to lose herself again inside her aches, pains, and forgetfulness. But it was creeping back. She couldn't keep the world out there at bay for very much longer.

"Did she say anything about the play?" she asked her mother.

"No, she didn't, darling," said her mother tenderly, "and I didn't ask her."

Her mother knew everything. That first terrible night before the fever and the aches and pains had mercifully shut her down, she had spilled it all out as she lay wrapped up, weeping, inside her mother's arms. She knew that her mother would feel the same kind of outrage she did over Ms. Drumm's assassination of *Romeo and Juliet,* and the same disappointment over Mrs. Kronberger's failure to get involved. Her mother had said something like, "Well, she doesn't know everything," when Beebe had related the teacher's obvious incredulity over her hopes of becoming an actress.

That was long ago it seemed. And Beebe tried to forget all the anguish and remember only how cozy it was here inside her home, alone with her mother. But the world was creeping back.

"I think I'll give up the play," Beebe said.

Her mother picked up her hand and pressed it. "Good idea," she said. "If it's being massacred, why be a part of it?"

"I think maybe I should forget about being an actress altogether," Beebe said carefully, and waited. She knew her mother would protest, would urge her to have patience, faith . . .

Her mother nodded. "Maybe that would be a good idea, Beebe. It's probably not worth all the rejections actors have to endure."

"You didn't have many rejections," Beebe said, almost accusingly.

Her mother patted her hand but remained silent.

"Why did you keep encouraging me?" Beebe asked, angry for the first time since her illness began.

"Because you wanted it so much," said her mother.

"No, no," Beebe cried, pulling her hand away. "It was because you wanted it. I did it for you. I always knew I wasn't any good. Well, maybe I didn't consciously know it, but deep down, I knew it."

Her mother stroked her hand. "Well, it doesn't matter anymore, Beebe. What's important is that now you can concentrate on your other interests."

"What other interests?" Beebe asked. "I don't have any other interests."

Her mother smiled. She was looking very pretty

tonight, Beebe noticed. She was also wearing her green Laura Ashley dress. "You have lots of other interests," said her mother fondly. "Shakespeare and books and poetry. You're a smart girl and you're generous and loving." Her mother cocked her head to one side and looked at her. "You're also a pretty girl, Beebe, and who knows . . ."

"I'm not interested in boys," Beebe muttered, and in her mind, Dave Mitchell, dressed in the purple velvet jerkin and black tights of Romeo, whispered in her ear, "It is my lady; O, it is my love!" And she half smiled at him and half frowned at her mother.

"Oh, you will be, you will be," her mother said confidently. She looked at her watch and stood up. "It's nearly six. I'd better take down the garbage."

"You look all dressed up today," Beebe said, settling back on her pillow. "Is Jim coming over tonight?"

"No," said her mother emphatically, "no, he's not."

"He's a nice man," Beebe said. "Too bad we couldn't make it over to his house for dinner last week."

"Beebe," said her mother, "I've broken up with Jim. Last night, I guess it was. Over the phone."

"But why, Mom? I thought you liked him."

"I do, Beebe, I do. It's just . . . I like him as a friend, and he's been, well, pressing me." She sat down again next to Beebe. "I mean, I've just started going out again, having fun. I'm not ready to commit myself to anybody, especially—well, he really is a darling, but we don't have the same interests." She looked at her watch again and leaped up. "I've got to take the garbage down."

"What's the big hurry about taking down the garbage?" Beebe asked.

"I'll tell you when I get back." There was a funny little giggle in her mother's voice as she hurried out of the room.

She was gone nearly an hour. In that time, Beebe got up from the couch, took a shower, and examined her face in the mirror. Was she pretty as her mother said? No, she didn't think so. Especially not now with her skin so pale and her face so thin. She ran a comb through her short, curly hair, and wondered what Dave Mitchell thought of her face. Did he think she was pretty?

She changed into a blue sweat suit, and, feeling tired, sank gratefully back down on the couch. She knew that the illness was past, and that she had some decisions to make soon. But for the time being, for the next day or so at any rate, she could forget everything unpleasant and lose herself inside her mother's total attention.

She could hear voices outside the door, laughter, then a key in the lock, and her mother's quick footsteps across the small foyer. Her mother's face was pink and her eyes bright as she came back into the living room.

"What is it, Mom?" Beebe asked. "What's happened? You look so happy."

"Oh, it's all so silly, and so . . . so marvelous," said her mother, sitting down again on the edge of the couch. "You know I usually take the garbage down in the morning before going to work. Or you take it before going to school. But you got sick last Thursday night, and I've been home with you ever since. Let's see." Her mother raised a hand and began counting on her fingers. "So the first night was Friday. I skipped Saturday, so the second was Sunday, then Monday, Tuesday, and tonight. So what's that? Just five nights." Her mother laughed and shook her head. "What a world!" she exclaimed. "What a wonderful, crazy world!"

"What happened, Mom?" Beebe asked uncomfortably. Her mother had changed, whatever had happened. Everything kept on changing and changing, but now, with her mother also part of the change, Beebe could feel something like terror. It grew and spun around in her head, and she lay back on the pillows and listened.

"Well, both of us got to the garbage can at the same time on Friday, and he was so funny. He held up the lid for me, and said something about tipping his lid to a lady. I don't remember exactly how he put it, but I couldn't help laughing. And we just chatted a little on the way up the stairs. So, I didn't take the garbage down on Saturday, but, sure enough, he was there on Sunday. I kind of had the feeling he might have been hanging around, waiting. Well, one thing led to another and—he lives in apartment 2C, on the landing

• 122 •

below ours. His name is Roland Belfiglio. He's a writer. Not famous or anything, and he works as a translator. He speaks Italian and Spanish fluently, and he admires Shakespeare. Only he thinks *King Lear* is the best. Well, so I told him tonight maybe I might be able to go to the movies with him this weekend if you're feeling better. We both want to see the new *Henry V* movie even if neither of us is crazy about the play. Incidentally, he thinks Dante is the greatest poet who ever lived, but I don't really mind."

Beebe sat in one of the back rows in the auditorium and watched. Juliet/Jennifer, wearing a short, flippy skirt and waving a green and black pom-pom, was leading a group of other cheerleaders in a cry—"Give me a *C*, give me a *C*, give me an *A*, give me an *A*. . . ."

"Louder!" ordered Ms. Drumm from one of the front rows. "And Romeo, get over there, behind the billboard, and act like you're really swept off your feet."

Romeo/Dave, chewing gum and dressed in a red-and-white school jacket with the word *Montague* stamped on the back, slouched over to the billboard and assumed a casual, sneering stance.

"Okay, girls, show him your stuff," said Ms. Drumm, sinking back into her seat.

The cheerleaders fanned out in a line behind Juliet, all of them waving green and black pom-poms. "Give me a *C*, give me a *C*. . . ." they cried, pumping their arms up and down and stamping their feet on the ground.

Romeo/Dave, peeping through a hole in the billboard, suddenly rose, straightened up, and spit out his gum. He walked around the side of the billboard as all of the cheerleaders leaped into the air yelling, "*Capulet!*"

"Good, good!" Ms. Drumm said.

Then Juliet caught sight of Romeo and slowly moved towards him, and he moved towards her. Off stage could be heard the cries of the cheerleaders from Montague High School as they, in turn, shouted, "Give me an *M*, give me an *M*. . . ."

Dave was the first one from the cast whom she saw on her return to school that morning. He came up to her in the hall and asked, "Were you away for a couple of days?"

"I was sick for nearly a week and a half," she told him.

"No kidding? Well, you've really missed something great. She's a kick, that Drumm, and we're having a ball."

"I guess nobody circulated a petition or went to the principal."

"Oh!" Dave made a face. "We're lucky nobody did. The play is really fun now. Everybody loves it. It's so cute and the lines are so easy."

"Everybody?" Beebe asked.

"Everybody," he assured her. "But you'd better go and check with Ms. Drumm about your part. I don't have a mother in this version. Probably she'll want you to be one of the cheerleaders. You'd make a cute one."

He gave her shoulder a friendly pat and went off.

Went off out of her life and out of her heart, she thought as she watched him amble up to Juliet on stage, and saw both of them exchange a high five.

Nothing was the same. Nothing in the play remained except for the rivalry between two high schools, Capulet and Montague, and the names of the characters. All the parts had changed. Most of the boys were now players on one of the two football teams, and most of the girls were cheerleaders. Over the phone last night, Wanda had prepared her for the worst.

"I'm still Juliet's mother and Frank Jackson is her father, but everything else is different. Even the nurse. She's Juliet's best friend now, and everything ends up happy at the end. Capulet High School wins the football game, but Montague High School gets the prize for the best cheerleaders. Or maybe it's the other way around."

"I'm dropping out," Beebe told Wanda.

"Look," Wanda said, "just come in and see what's going on. It won't hurt you to look. Maybe you'll love it, too, the way the rest of us do."

"I know I won't."

"Oh you, you're such a snob. Just come and look . . . and . . . and Beebe, there's something else."

"What?"

"Well, you know that guy I wanted to fix you up with."

"Oh, yes. It's okay now. I wouldn't mind meeting him."

"Well, that's just it. I don't know. Maybe he's going through something, but he just called me and said he didn't want to."

"Didn't want to what?"

"Well—meet you. But I'll talk to him again. He just might be shy. Anyway, I'll see you tomorrow in the auditorium."

She did see Wanda, but Wanda didn't see her. Wanda was walking out of the auditorium, hand in hand with Frank. They were so absorbed in each other that they passed Beebe's row, only a few yards away, without seeing her there.

I'm invisible, Beebe thought to herself. Even Wanda doesn't know I'm here. I'm invisible and unimportant, and I'm all alone now in the back of this terrible auditorium, where up front people are murdering my favorite play right before my eyes.

"I think," Ms. Drumm called out, "we'd better do that scene again. Some of the cheerleaders aren't really getting into it. Let's start all over again. Romeo, get behind the billboard and start chewing your gum."

How could she ever have been so dotty over Dave Mitchell, slouching there behind the billboard, chewing gum and peeping through the peephole at Juliet. She saw him now as he was, an ordinary, uninteresting, shallow boy whom she had endowed with special qualities.

"Thy love did read by rote, and could not spell," she whispered to herself. But the wonderful lines did not make her feel better as they usually did.

To have everything change around her all at once was too much. She would never be an actress, she knew it now. The play was dead, and she, in the back of the auditorium, sat helplessly by as its murderers cavorted on stage in front of her. And her mother—changed and cheerful. Wanda in love. Dave Mitchell, completely gone from her life.

What was left? A future that was uncertain, a whole whirling world of questions with no answers, and a terrible, empty loneliness. She needed somebody to talk to, somebody who could understand. She needed, she needed . . .

But it was only in books that miracles happened, that two kindred souls met by chance, that Romeo emerged from out of the shadows to declare his love for Juliet. The tears rolled down her face and fell on her hands, folded helplessly in her lap.

His father took it hard.

"One day, we're making plans, and the next, she's telling me it's all over. What did I do? What did I say?"

Mark tried to be supportive. "You didn't say anything, Dad. Don't blame yourself."

"It was because of that kid of hers. Just because she was sick. I called every day. I tried to help out, but she didn't let me do anything."

"Well, maybe she was just upset because her daughter was sick. Maybe when she's better . . ."

"No, no," his father said. "Her daughter is better. She's going back to school tomorrow. I called her a few minutes ago. I said let's get together—just to talk, but she said no. She said there was no point in talking.

I bet it was her kid. I bet it was Beebe who bad-mouthed me.''

"But Dad, you said she was a nice girl. You said she liked you.''

"I thought she did, but then I remember on Angel Island, she was the one who started talking about Shakespeare. That's right. She started it, and then that got Barbara going, and then she asked me what I thought. I guess she was trying to show me up—the jealous little snob. She knew her mother was going with me, and she couldn't stand it. That's why she broke it up.''

"But Dad, maybe it was something else.'' Mark could feel the disappointment rising inside of him.

"No,'' said his father. "It was that Beebe. She was the one.''

He had to harden his heart later when he called Wanda. Any enemy of his father, he decided, had to be an enemy of his.

"Hello, Wanda,'' he said. "It's Mark.''

"Hi, Mark, I was going to give you a ring tonight.''

"Well, I just wanted to tell you . . .''

"Beebe's coming back to school tomorrow. I'll call her after I finish talking to you. We can set something up for this weekend. Friday's fine with Frank and me, or Saturday . . .''

"Well, something's come up.''

"Well, Sunday's okay. We could walk across the bridge to Sausalito on Sunday, if you like, and take the ferry back. Beebe likes to hike.''

"No," he said painfully. His father's enemies were his enemies, and if this mean, snobbish girl had really been responsible for his father's anguish, he didn't want to have anything to do with her. "I can't come this weekend. I mean, let's just call the whole thing off."

"Did you meet somebody else?" Wanda asked.

"No, but . . ."

"But what?"

"Look, I just don't want to. That's all."

"Why not?"

"I don't want to."

"Why don't you just meet her? I really think you'd like her, and I think she'd like you too. You both really have a lot in common."

"Like what?" he couldn't help asking. "Isn't she a Shakespeare nut? Isn't she in that acting group of yours?"

"Well, yes and no," Wanda said. "She is crazy about Shakespeare, but I don't think she'll be in our play. She's a serious girl, too serious, I think, for her own good. I mean, in a nice way. I mean, she doesn't run with the crowd, but in a nice way. And, Mark, she's pretty, and you can talk to her and she really listens."

"No," he said quickly. Beebe sounded wonderful. "No. I've changed my mind."

"Well, let's talk about it in school tomorrow." She laughed. "I'm not letting you off the hook so easily."

He purposely cut his history class because Wanda was in it. There was no point in talking to her about why he wouldn't—couldn't—meet Beebe Clarke. His father's enemies were his enemies. And yet, he couldn't help wondering if his father was mistaken. Perhaps it didn't have anything at all to do with Beebe or with Shakespeare. As much as he loved his father, he couldn't help seeing some of his faults and how demanding he was of Barbara. Oh, he supposed, most people who were in love wanted to spend all their time, or at least most of it, with the person they loved. He supposed his father must have been like most people in love. But if he was, then maybe there was something wrong with being in love.

It hadn't happened to him yet, but he felt love should open doors and not close them. It should make your life bigger and not smaller. It shouldn't lock you into a cramped space but take you out into a universe filled with new stars and brighter constellations. One day, he knew, it would happen to him, and he wished it would happen soon.

That's when he saw her. Wanda. Coming out of one of the side doors of the auditorium. She was laughing up into the face of some guy. In desperation he ducked into the auditorium through one of the doors on the other side. His heart was pounding, and he leaned against the door and waited. Waited for his heart to stop beating so hard, and also for a few minutes to pass. It would be safe in a few minutes for him to leave his sanctuary without danger of bumping into Wanda.

What a racket was going on in the auditorium! He turned his eyes to the stage up front, where a whole bunch of girls in cheerleader outfits were leaping up and down and yelling "Give me a *C,* give me a *C*" at the top of their lungs. He couldn't help noticing that they weren't very good and were completely out of step. Some of them were stamping on the ground, while others were leaping into the air. And they were waving pom-poms in the craziest, wildest way. It was deafening, and he turned to leave when he noticed her.

Over towards the middle, a few rows down. Her head was bent over her hands, her shoulders were heaving, and she was sobbing. A girl was crying in the back of the auditorium. He could actually hear her, in spite of the din from the stage.

And he could feel her sadness. How strange that he could feel it, as he had felt it himself just a few days ago up on the top of Twin Peaks. She was crying the way he had cried. All by herself with nobody to notice or to care. Something had gone wrong for her the way it had for him.

"It will be all right," he needed to tell her. "It will pass, whatever it is, and it will be all right."

He moved towards her, and as he approached she suddenly turned around and raised her face up to his. Her face was wet with tears. He sat down next to her, and saw two images of himself reflected inside the circles of her eyes. Up on the stage, the cheerleaders bellowed *"Capulet, Capulet,"* as he leaned towards her and began to speak.